SARAH VERNON

Drawn to Murder

Contents

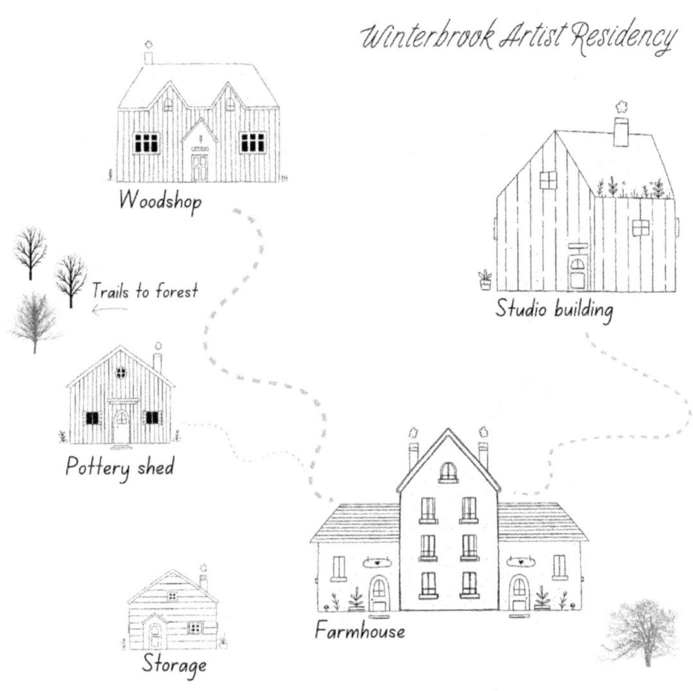

Winterbrook Artist Residency
Woodshop
Trails to forest
Pottery shed
Storage
Studio building
Farmhouse
Boston, 250 miles

1

Chapter 1

"**S**am, it's your turn."

I jolted out of my daydreaming, looking up at the dark-eyed, even darker-haired man across from me at the table. From the intensity of his expectant stare, you'd think we were plotting world domination, not playing a simple getting-to-know-you game. If you could call revealing unexpected or odd facts about yourself a game. Everyone was just trying to one up each other in achievements, fame or outright weirdness - because this was a group of artists, after all.

"Uh, sure. I'm Sam. Samantha, but everyone calls me Sam," I said, stumbling over my words and sure that my cheeks were as bright red as they felt. Whatever I had been planning to say was instantly forgotten. Was there anyone who actually enjoyed these kinds of introductions?

"I'm here from Boston," I continued. "I just graduated from school in the spring and I'm…taking a kind of gap year at the moment. I primarily work in ceramics and sculpture, especially miniatures." I paused, willing anyone else to make a comment or ask a question, anything to save me from having to think of an interesting fact to share. What was there to say that was appropriate for this group? I grew up in New York? I have a cat named Paul? I once tripped over the body of a dead famous sculptor who'd been poisoned?

There were polite smiles around the table, which I returned, slightly nodding my head, signaling that I was done with my intro. I was saved from further humiliation-by-spotlight by the woman on my right, who moved her wheelchair closer to the table so everyone could see her.

"I'm Tony. Tonya, but everyone calls me Tony," she said, throwing a small smile my way. "I'm here from LA, where I make immersive installations that challenge viewers' perceptions of their interactions with, and limitations within, the physical world." Tony waited a beat, tilting her chin as if daring any of us to ask the obvious question. There were more polite smiles, although I noticed about half of our group were studiously avoiding eye contact.

Unfortunately, only Eliot took the bait. "What inspired you towards that kind of work?" he asked with a kind of forced obliviousness. I didn't think any of us needed more of an introduction to Eliot: over the course of the previous twenty-four hours since we'd gotten to the Winterbrook Artist Residency, he'd made himself known as the type of pompous, arrogant artist that gives the rest of us a bad name.

"Well, Eliot," Tony said, returning his tone. "I've used a wheelchair since I was a kid, after a spinal injury. So after all these years experiencing a very different side of the physical world, I thought I'd give other people the chance to have a similar view." The pair politely smiled at each other (although, one did have to admit - and admire - that Tony's smile had more than a hint of crocodile to it) while the rest of us avoided engaging. "But if you'll forgive me, I think I'll actually head up to bed now," Tony said, wheeling away from the table. "It was great to meet all of you!" she called cheerily as she turned towards the door, her wheelchair making an unmistakable bumping motion over Eliot's foot as she left. I couldn't help but grin.

*

It was now the deepest, coldest part of a New England winter and I had been at loose ends since I had graduated in the spring. I'd worked a string of random jobs all summer, moving from one gallery to the next, always perched behind an identical white reception desk to answer phones and hand out gallery brochures and price lists all day, the whole time promising myself that something better would come along soon. All night I would work in the studio, sending out images of my work to any gallery I could think of, and completing page after page of grant applications for any program that seemed even remotely relevant: grants for women artists, grants for young artists, grants for artists who worked in mixed media, grants for artists whose names begin with an S (I mean, not really, but that was as crazily specific as some of the programs could get). But as the summer gradually became the fall, I had to admit to myself that my timeline for something better might have been wrong.

The one bright spot was Arun. We'd started dating during my junior year, and now that I had so much time on my hands, it was easy to distract myself with - I mean, focus on our relationship.

In fact, he was the one who'd suggested I try this residency program, tucked away in northern Vermont. Arun mentioned it one night when I was sitting in my kitchen, watching him cook dinner. As he stood at the stove, studiously stirring and avoiding my look, he told me about a woman he'd gone to school with, who was now on the Board of Directors of an artists' residency program.

"Can't wait to get me out of your hair?" I joked, my casual tone cover for what was really my instant enthusiasm. I pulled up the Winterbrook Residency's website on my phone, taking in the images of a rustic farmhouse set in a gorgeous landscape of old farmland and new forest, with artists busily creating masterpieces all over the place, as is their wont.

"Of course not, Sam," Arun said, "You know it's not like that. I just think it could be good for you. Just to get away for a while, have something else to look at besides another January in Boston. Plus, I'm only bringing it up because I saw she posted that an artist just dropped out at the last minute, so they have an open spot for the next residency cycle. If you want, I'm happy to get in touch with her."

I promised I'd think about it, even though I already knew my answer would be yes. I'd be lying if I said I hadn't instantly started planning what I could work on there, with a free three weeks and access to their facilities. And realistically, I had started to go a bit stir crazy these past few weeks. It was when I suggested we play a game I'd devised based on *The Real Inspector Hound* - kind of a murder mystery party crossed with charades - that Arun brought up the residency. It was my fault for underselling the game. I had started the conversation with "Do you know what'd be fun?" And, as we all know, the answer is almost never the thing the person is about to suggest.

*

So now, instead of sitting at home playing a cozy murder game, I was sitting at a table full of artists introducing themselves. After Eliot, we'd heard from Simon, a photographer from New York who worked as a product photographer for an ad agency, but was here for the chance to work out his more creative ideas, and Ryan, a quiet woodworker from somewhere near Chicago who had about as much to say about himself as I had.

"And so that's really what led me to this work, with historical maps overlaid with personal drawings and different textual objects," Brandon was saying as he passed his phone around the table, making sure we all saw the work in question. He was a tall, slim man with the kind of eternally youthful look that just wasn't fair. I smiled politely as the phone was passed to me, wondering what Stephanie, my best friend back in Boston, would have to say about these drawings. She was the only one of us who hadn't gone to art school - which meant she was usually the one who could look at things like this with the clearest eyes. And the snarkiest (and honestly funniest) tone.

"Amazing," Evan cooed, handing the phone back to Brandon. "I love all the different layers you're able to get into such small pieces." I tried hard not to roll my eyes, instead looking around the table to gauge everyone else's thoughts. It wasn't that his work was bad; in fact, technically, it was certainly well made. It was just that I couldn't help but cringe a bit whenever I heard anyone speak at such lengths about their work, and unfortunately this usually started to reflect on the work itself. From their expressions, it seemed like about half the room was team Brandon. It was no surprise that this included Evan: he and Brandon had instantly hit it off, becoming basically inseparable from the first day. Evan, an abstract painter, was like an even more petite version of Brandon, with a similar mop of light brown hair, falling just so.

As Brandon finished smiling away everyone's compliments, our attention turned to the woman next to him.

"I'm Rachel," she drawled in a way that made me wonder whether she really spelled it with extra letters or was just adding a few more syllables for effect. "I'm here from L.A.," she nodded to her fellow Angelinos at the table. "I work in fiber arts, primarily, combining weaving and quilting techniques with painting. Although I'm here because I'd really like to push my work sculpturally. Really build out the surface of the work into a deeper dimension." We explored what this could look like for a few minutes, while I wondered if I should have said more about my own work. In school, I'd practically lived in the pottery studio, forming the kind of muscle memory at the pottery wheel that only comes from years of daily use. Without regular access to a wheel and kiln, my work had floundered a bit since then, becoming more unruly as I tried different materials and new techniques. But I guess it was all in the spin. Instead of unruly, I could've called it "a new exploration," in which I "utilized new multimedia approaches." That sounded better than "I usually find interesting stuff in the trash and try to cobble things together from my bedroom-slash-studio, like some kind of arty, feminine version of Victor Frankenstein."

Although it seemed like the next artist to introduce himself might approve of my trash approach.

"Timothy," he said, brushing back shaggy blonde hair as he spoke - although his was a mop much less artful than Evan's or Brandon's. I wondered if he was single, knowing I probably wouldn't let Arun get away without a haircut for that long. "I work as a painter, mostly, with some sculpture. Although professionally, I've done a lot of jobs in the arts: carpenter, art handler, mover." He exchanged manly nods with Ryan, who had a similar career path. "And I'm from Western Massachusetts."

"I don't know how you can live with this much snow all the time!" Eliot cried dramatically. Probably just making sure we all remembered he, too, was from LA.

Jenny rolled her eyes. "It's not all the time, *Eliot*," she said, somehow able to make his name sound like a curse word. "Anyway, I'm Jenny. From Queens, New York City. And I also work as a painter, doing mostly portraits at the moment."

I'd already met Jenny, as we were somehow two of the only smokers in a group of artists, so naturally we'd had a bit of a bonding moment to start with. Out of everyone, her work had quickly emerged as my favorite: she painted bold, colorful portraits that were balanced perfectly on the edge of being a kind of Pop Art-y illustration. Much as I like her work, I appreciated Jenny's brevity now. It was getting late, and I could practically hear the flannel sheets upstairs calling to me. Taking my cue from Tony, I made my excuses and headed up. Unfortunately, I didn't have my own wheelchair to do more damage to Eliot's toes.

*

The first few days passed by in a blur of 'new school year' feeling and figuring out where everything was on the sprawling old farm. "Isolated" and "remote" barely cut it. We were about as close to Canada as you could get without a passport, far away from the noise of any highway or even much of a town. After growing up in a commuter suburb near New York City, and then four years in the middle of Boston, the silence around the farmhouse was deafening - an oxymoron I'd never really experienced before. It wasn't even silence, when you really started to pay attention: who knew wind could whistle through trees this loudly? Even the snow seemed to creak as noisily as the stairs in our old apartment building back in Boston.

My room was tucked up on the second floor of the farmhouse, a misnomer for what was really a sprawling Victorian mansion that some enterprising family had added onto at least once each decade since it was initially built. Spread out around the house were a series of outbuildings, including a beautiful new, light-filled studio building that appeared purpose-built for the painters in the group. Ryan spent most of his time in the woodshop next door, occasionally joined by Timothy, while poor Simon was confined to a basement darkroom, built underneath the studio building - although even the basement facility was pretty state-of-the-art. Personally, I spent my time moving between each building, taking in the musty, rusty smells of a storage shed full of supplies before picking my way through scrap materials in the wood shop, eventually, inevitably, ending up in the pottery shed.

I quickly settled into a routine. Each morning, I'd set off with a thermos of coffee and take a small, barely passable trail into the forest surrounding the farmhouse. We were near the border of a large state park, but this small offshoot of forest was just rugged enough to be shockingly beautiful, but not so rugged that my city legs couldn't hack it - even if, on more than one occasion already, I'd gotten turned around trying to find my way on the leaf covered trail, which could quickly become invisible if you ventured a few steps off course. As I walked, I'd scan the ground like a magpie, trying not to look so much as letting things catch my eye. (Yes, just the way I'd learned in a freshman year class that, if I remember correctly, was called "Intro to Looking.") The trail was covered with half-rotting leaves and twigs splayed out between rocks, the snow receding just enough to let the fall colors show through. At first, I'd considered my collecting to be just another form of procrastinating. But the more I looked at the golden yellow triangles of birch leaves, the gnarled twigs falling from the old apple trees, and the scratchy stalks of last year's goldenrod, the more I realized there may really be something to all this. The mini bonfire I was putting together in the pottery shed reminded me of the technique of raku firing, in which a piece comes straight out of the kiln and gets tucked into a pile of combustible materials. Since the piece is still molten hot, all the leaves, twigs, or straw instantly start to burn. The burning materials create unpredictable patterns on the ceramic, with sometimes unique colors that can be hard to achieve with regular glazes. It seemed like a fitting metaphor for this gap year of mine: unpredictable, a bit more out of control than I'd really like to admit. I hadn't tried raku since my first intro to pottery class when I was a freshman, but I figured that was the whole point of residencies like this: trying new things. Or new old things. You know what I mean.

*

It was mid-morning as I got back from my usual walk and opened the door to the pottery shed. It was a bit bigger than your average garden shed, but not much more finished: its walls were still unfinished wood and though the room was filled with sturdy desks, drying racks, and almost new pottery wheels, the space still had major log cabin vibes. Mercifully, as the only ceramics artist in the bunch, the small space was all mine. As I switched on the overhead lights, I took a moment to appreciate the smell, an earthy mix of wet clay and old wood. My ideal perfume, in other words.

I sat down at the wheel, rolling my sleeves up and, without stopping to think, dipped into the huge chunk of plastic-wrapped clay at my feet and deftly cut a hunk off with a wire loop tool. Wetting my hands and a sponge, I fixed the clay onto the wheel (which took something of a hard slam that still never came elegantly to me) and slowly started up the foot pedal. It was easy to go into a kind of trance at this point, half watching the clay as it spun, mesmerized as new shapes emerged at the slightest touch, and half moving only by feel, allowing my hands to make their own decisions, aware that the smallest differences in pressure and angle could take the piece into wildly different directions. I thought back to the introductions we heard on Monday night, shaking my head at the memory. How could you possibly put this experience into adequate words? It was my idea of heaven. Little did I know how much I should've been appreciating these moments here, savoring this time while it lasted. Because soon, it would all be over.

2

Chapter 2

By Saturday, it seemed like everyone had relaxed enough to put down whatever pretentious, artistic guards had been up, and we could finally hang out somewhat more normally and casually. Tony, Simon, Jenny and I were in the living room, playing some impenetrable board game about making wine that I was only pretending to understand (I do a good "thoughtful decision making" face, or at least I hoped I did), while Brandon, Evan and Rachel lounged on the couches behind us. Warm from the crackling fire we'd started in the old brick fireplace (yes, truly crackling) - and more so from the homemade mead that Simon had so thoughtfully decided to pack - Timothy's entrance jolted us out of our stupor.

"Where is it?" he demanded, barging in. "My sketchbook. Who took it?" No one moved, aside from a few heads turning as he stood towering in the doorway. Brandon was the first to speak.

"Sorry, no idea," he said. "Where did you last see it?"

"If it was where I last saw it, would I be standing here right now?" Timothy growled. Brandon threw up his hands in defense.

"Chill, man. I have no idea where your book is. Just trying to help." Brandon sank back onto the couch, clearing giving up any pretense of helping. The rest of us exchanged uneasy looks as Timothy stood there, waiting for answers.

"Sorry, Tim. But I haven't seen it either," Jenny offered. "From your look, I'm guessing you already searched for it?"

Timothy sighed. "Yeah, of course. Look, I'm sorry to storm in here like this. It's just…starting to get weird."

An uneasy silence descended on the room, slowly turning the small space from cozy to claustrophobic.

"If it helps, I'm sure I just left my iron at home," Jenny said. There were nods of agreement throughout the living room.

"Yeah, I definitely think I left the paints at home, too. I mean, probably." Evan chimed in. Despite these reassurances, it was hard to dispel the sense of unease that had blown in. The truth was, the first few days hadn't been totally without incidence. A few things had gone missing: Jenny's iron, a couple bottles of paint pigments from Evan. And now Timothy's sketchbook. In my mind, I pictured Nancy Drew opening up a fresh notebook, ready to record clues - then pictured snapping said notebook shut and erased any such thoughts from my mind, wishing myself firmly back into place in my tranquil pottery studio mindset.

"It's just weird. I mean, who cares about someone else's sketch-book?" Tony asked. "The paints I guess I could understand, since pigments can be pretty pricey. But a used sketchbook?" she paused, thoughtfully rolling the dice in her hand, as if we were going to be able to keep playing after this.

"Unless it was empty?" she asked, with a note of hope. Timothy shook his head.

"Nope, not even close. It was an old book, pretty much full," he sighed. "Anyway, you guys are right. I'm sure I just misplaced it and am overreacting. Sorry about that, just forget it. I'll keep looking." With that, he lopped off, leaving the room quiet. The dice clattered noisily as Tony dropped them onto the table, moving her cards with exaggerated enthusiasm.

I had to agree with Timothy: the missing stuff was definitely getting weird. A hushed smoke break conversation with Jenny a couple days before, after the paints had quickly followed her missing iron, confirmed that she didn't, in fact, think she'd left it at home and had definitely seen it when unpacking on Monday. She just didn't want to make a big deal of it.

"This isn't my first residency," she'd said, "I mean, nothing like this has ever happened, like supplies getting stolen. But I know how cliquey these things can get, and how quickly. I didn't want to be that person, and just instantly start complaining or accusing strangers." I agreed and could see where she was coming from. This may have been my first residency, but you didn't need to tell me about how quickly allegiances could form among strangers, often set off by the smallest things.

I tried to return my attention to the board game, but couldn't shake the feeling that there may be more to this than simply misplaced objects. From the obvious tension in the room, I didn't think I was the only one feeling this way. Even the two tittering love birds on the couch behind me had suddenly gone quiet.

Into this gloom stepped Madeline Berry, letting us know that dinner would be ready soon. Compared to Timothy's march in here, her entrance was more like a cat slinking in. And like a cat, it seemed she could take us or leave us. But I had to imagine that when you applied to be the caretaker of an artist's residency program, you knew what you were signing up for. I wondered if anyone had mentioned the missing materials to her, making a mental note to ask her - before I caught myself. None of my things had gone missing. I didn't need to get involved. I threw the dice, looking across the game board in what I hoped looked like quiet contemplation, but which was really plain confusion. If only I knew what my next move should be.

*

I headed back out to the pottery shed after a quiet dinner. Even Jenny and Brandon's playful sparring over whether New York or L.A. had better restaurants couldn't fully lighten the mood. I was grateful to escape outside after the meal, settling in at the wheel once again and propping my phone up next to me on an old wooden table that may or may not have once been someone's cutting board.

"Hi, love," Arun answered. I wondered when I would stop having that nervous flutter of anticipation each time I heard him answer. "How're you doing up there in the freezing north?"

"Right, cause it's so balmy in Boston? Didn't I hear that you guys are the ones getting another foot of snow this weekend?"

Arun laughed. "Yeah, touché. But really, you doing okay?" I heard him sip something in the background, and could just picture him: covering for Steph in their family's grocery store, enjoying a beer behind the counter in the quiet moments between customers.

"Everything's fine here," I said, revving up the wheel and hoping the sound drowned out any undertones in my voice.

"Really burning the midnight oil, it sounds like," Arun said.

"You know me. Free reign in a new pottery shed? Like catnip to an artist."

"That's great, Sam. I'm glad you're enjoying it. Just hope you're getting enough time to relax a bit, too. Making new friends?" I chose not to hear the 'yet' in his last question. I felt like a kid at summer camp being questioned by their parents, and said as much.

"Fair enough," Arun laughed. "Moving on."

"Dare I ask how work is going?" I said as I flattened my hands over the ball of clay on the wheel, pushing it down into a shallow disc. I never got tired of the feeling of smooth clay slipping easily in my hands, the speed with which new forms could take shape.

On the phone, Arun groaned. "Maybe don't ask," he said. "It's a break just to cover for Steph in the store tonight." I smiled as my hunch about his evening plans was confirmed.

Despite these protests, Arun proceeded to give me a run down of his work week. He'd been covering a major murder trial for his paper, and while he'd written about a series of big cases as a journalist previously (only two of which involved yours truly), the scale of this investigation was really kicking his butt. Even with my love of puzzles, I couldn't quite follow all the threads of organized crime, petty jealousy, and investigator mishaps. I could almost see the television crews that were surely materializing along the sidelines already, ready to make the next true crime docuseries - in which, I could pretty confidently guess, Arun would not want a starring role.

"It's going to drag on for the next few weeks, at least," Arun said. "Probably even more. Apparently, the state only just found new evidence that, if you were to believe every single thing their press officer says, is so crucial it'll provide an airtight case for the prosecution."

"So crucial they only just found it?" I asked.

"Exactly," Arun laughed. "That's pretty much what I said. But apparently, it was this accounting ledger that had been taped to the underside of a boat, in some kind of waterproof bag."

"Which they found how, exactly?" I replied. "Probably with the help of some tourists on a duck boat, I'm sure."

Arun laughed. "Yep, I'm sure that's exactly how it happened." Although his tone was light, I could still hear the exhaustion in his voice.

"I'm sorry, honey," I said, more serious now. "Is there any indication of when you might get a break?" I had been hoping Arun might be able to come up for a visit next weekend, but it didn't sound likely now.

"No idea, unfortunately," Arun said. "My contact at the prosecutor's office had said they may be able to start winding down in the next few weeks, but that was before this new evidence came up." I heard the faint tinkle of a bell in the background as the door to the store opened.

"Sorry, Sam, but I should go. Talk tomorrow?" We signed off and I tapped my phone off with a clay-covered finger, leaving a vague gray smudge on the screen. I was still picturing Arun at the counter, making small talk with the customer, probably a regular, his beer tucked away out of sight. Smiling at the familiar image, I got back to work.

*

I spent most of Sunday in the same position, moving between

the pottery wheel and the kiln, pausing only to stretch and take a coffee break. Right now, given where the dinner conversation was currently heading, I was regretting leaving the shed at all.

"I'm just saying, it's not bad to have options," Brandon was saying, as he gestured with a forkful of pasta at Simon.

"Never hurts to have a steady job, though," Ryan cut in from down the table, with Timothy nodding his agreement. Talk about plans for the next week had quickly turned to plans in general, and what everyone planned on doing after our three weeks here were up. I'd so far successfully avoided thinking about the topic myself, secretly dreading the cold white gallery desk that was waiting for me in Boston.

"Listen, it's not a decision I have to make right away. This was just supposed to be a little trial run," Simon said. When he mentioned possibly leaving his job at an ad agency to pursue working as an artist full-time, the group had erupted into a lively debate over the merits of day job versus creative freedom.

"Personally, I think a bit of both is the right way to go," Tony chimed in. "I have a permanent part-time job doing museum education work; it's stable, a good enough paycheck, and it leaves me plenty of time on the side for everything else."

"Thanks, everyone. I'll be sure to take all this under advisement," Simon said with a barely concealed eye roll, clearly as ready as I was for a new topic of conversations. He turned his attention back to his plate.

"Whatever, Si. I think it's always good to go for the big change," Brandon said. "Be bold."

"Couldn't agree more," Eliot added. He'd been conspicuously quiet all through dinner but I knew he wouldn't be able to resist chiming in for long.

"Oh, yeah? So what big, bold change are you planning, Eliot?" I didn't know why Brandon insisted on goading him at every opportunity, but it made me wonder if he was a younger sibling. The rest of us would be just as happy not to hear every little thing that Eliot was thinking.

"Well, I can't say all the details just yet," Eliot said coyly. "But, I'm thinking of starting a new business." He paused, clearly waiting for questions. Luckily, even Brandon wouldn't give him the satisfaction. I had to admit, the guy did have a pretty good sense of timing.

"It's in the fine art market. Or commercial art, if you will," Eliot went on, unbidden. "Working with blue-chip galleries and the like. In fact, maybe one of you could make frames for me?" Eliot looked at Timothy and Ryan expectantly, our resident woodworkers. I wasn't sure whether to call his expression a smirk or a sneer. It reminded me of languages that have dozens of words for snow or rain - this guy was ready made to inspire dozens of words for "smirk."

"Not much of a framer, myself," Ryan answered. "But I guess I'd be happy to help if you really needed someone."

"I got out of that work a while ago," Timothy said, returning Eliot's stare. "I quit art handling last year to focus on my own work. I only take on select jobs at the moment." Eliot stayed quiet, nodding.

"Okay, well," Brandon interrupted. Five minutes was too long for us not to be focused on him. I caught Tony laughing to herself across the table and grinned.

"If you could do anything at all, what would it be?" Brandon asked. "And don't say artist. Like, childhood dream job?" Talk quickly turned to fashion designers and astronauts, our actual plans mercifully dropped for now. I knew at some point I would need to face the future that sprawled out ahead of me, both tantalizingly and terrifyingly blank, but now didn't have to be that time. Not quite yet. I wanted to savor the rest of these three weeks while I could.

3

Chapter 3

The script was becoming all too familiar. As Rachel marched into the studio building on Monday afternoon, I could practically mouth the words alongside her as she demanded to know who had taken her roll of canvas, where it was now, and what she was going to do to whoever had taken it when she found it.

"Come on, guys," she said, "If this is a joke, it's getting really old." Rachel paused, glaring at each of us in turn. I shook my head at her stare, looking down to avoid looking at anyone else in the room. If I was being honest, I had to admit that I was starting to have my suspicions. Evan, playing all meek and mild? If he was brilliant, of course he'd steal his own paints to throw off suspicion. And Brandon, always the first to offer help? Come on. Suspicious as heck. If I were Rachel, I'd probably suspect me, too - the whole poor struggling artist act? Not really an act, in my case. I mean, I wasn't a painter, but I still knew how much a roll of canvas cost.

"Really," Rachel demanded, hands on her hips. "I didn't bring any more canvas with me. Now I'm going to have to wait days for more to get delivered."

"If anyone can even get through up here," Tony added helpfully, gesturing up to the skylights currently framing a threateningly gray sky.

"I'm really sorry, Rach, but I haven't seen a roll of canvas. The five of us have been in here all day," Brandon said, gesturing to myself, Tony, Jenny, and Evan. There were nods of agreement.

"Yeah, no one's even left all morning," Evan added, to more nods. Okay, so that wasn't entirely true. But I guess a normal person wouldn't be mentally documenting each smoke or bathroom break taken. Luckily, for the sake of the missing objects, I wasn't a normal person and could say with certainty that Jenny, Evan, and I had all left at some point. And obviously, it wasn't me.

"This is just so frustrating," Rachel said with a sigh. "I guess I just have to keep looking."

"We should organize a search party," Brandon said. "Find all this stuff once and for all. You know, fan out in a chain." Evan snickered quietly.

"It's not a missing child, Brandon," Jenny said. She turned her attention back to the old can of white paint at her feet, pausing to expertly tie up her long black hair before attacking the lid anew with a small crow bar.

Rachel left, silent except for one final stomp, a stomp made for the kind of big, empty, echoy barn we were in. I tried to turn back to my work, exchanging glances with Tony. She'd paused, thoughtful, staring blankly at the installation maquette she was working on.

"It really is getting old," Evan said, to no one and everyone. "And creepy. Plus, my paintings have been wrong all week. I'm not used to using colors straight out of the tube. I usually mix the pigments myself."

"Here, maybe this will help," Jenny said, offering up the now open can of white paint with just enough force that some sloshed over the side, landing near Evan's pristine boots. He cringed away.

"Thanks, but no thanks," Evan said. Jenny shrugged, hiding a grin as she turned back into her own studio cubicle. At least if Arun was going to nag me about making new friends, there were a few choice candidates here.

I debated whether I should text him about this latest object. I had tried to nonchalantly mention it, after the pigments had gone missing, and received an earful about staying out of trouble and minding my own business. I checked the time: Monday, eleven a.m. I could picture Arun sitting in the courtroom, laptop precariously balanced on his lap as he struggled with the story taking shape. Best not to bother him with this.

I shifted my chair so that I was facing the wall, blocking the other artists from view and trying to refocus. After a few early attempts with raku firing over the weekend had been promising, producing molten-looking blobs reminiscent of the forest floor that had inspired them, I'd decided they deserved some kind of stand or pedestal. Elevating the natural to the artistic, blah blah blah. I didn't want to read too much into it, at least not yet. It was a departure for me, from the work I'd spent years doing all through art school. There, I'd indulged my lifelong love of miniatures, crafting meticulous reproductions of historic pottery forms, never tiring of the way that ordinary, mundane objects could take on completely new lives in miniature. It felt a bit odd to me to be working like this, making these abstract forms - why? Just because I liked them, and I was interested in them. If I was being honest, it even felt a bit scary. No matter how long you've worked as an artist, I think it's always hard to say that you made something only because you were interested in making it.

In any event, I was in the studio building now to paint a few draft models of the stands for ceramics. Brushing on another coat of chalky black paint, I tried to keep my brushstrokes as delicate as possible, aware that the stand was starting to shake a bit. But I was too late. With only more brushstroke, the stand snapped apart at the corners. I looked down at the pile of wood on the desk, regretting not taking Ryan's advice about hide glue versus wood glue. Well, I reasoned, at least I had my afternoon's work cut out for me. After all, I'd quickly realized - with the help of Arun's slight nagging - that if I didn't keep my head down and focus on my own work, it would be all too easy to get sucked into everyone else's drama and the brouhaha brewing over the missing objects. It never ceased to amaze me how quickly artists could drum up so much drama.

*

After an afternoon (and, if I was honest, most of an evening) spent trying to clamp tiny pieces of wood together amid glue that was somehow simultaneously slippery and rapidly setting, I had a restless night. Falling asleep was easy enough. It was staying asleep that was the problem. Every hour, on cue, I was woken up by a sound from either inside or outside the house: creaking floorboards on the stairs, wind groaning through the attic rafters, or, most alarmingly, the sound of coyotes howling at a distance that seemed much, much too close to be safe. Staring at the dark ceiling, I smiled as I thought of what Rebecca, my roommate in Boston, would say. Normally the most level headed, calm, Mom of the bunch, Rebecca was always surprisingly quick to indulge her superstitious side. After a restless night like this, I could just see her tutting at me, sure that this was some kind of ominous sign. And not just the effect of living in cities most of my life, growing used to regular noises. Like, you know, traffic and people shouting and fire crackers.

I rolled over, checking the time on my phone and groaning as the display glared back at me, an alarmingly bright six a.m. Well, if I was already up, I may as well be up.

I dressed as quietly as I could, layering on both a heavy flannel shirt and an old wool varsity jacket. If I'd learned anything living through Boston winters, it was that it never hurt to look as much like an extra from *Twin Peaks* as possible.

I crept down the stairs and out the back door, making a beeline for the storage shed behind the house. Shed was a misnomer: It was really more of a small barn, with firewood stacked along the back wall and years of forgotten art supplies piled in front of and filling metal storage lockers. I pulled down the chain for the light, trying to ignore the creepy way the bare bulb swung, barely illuminating the far corners. At least I quickly found what I was looking for, and climbed over boxes of old canvases to reach a few bottles of glazes that I'd hidden - I mean, thoughtfully tucked away - behind one of the lockers.

Glaze in hand, I speed walked through the yard over to the wood shop, hoping that my re-made wooden stands had dried properly overnight. Under the humbly not-too-proud-of-himself gaze of Ryan, I had spent the rest of the day yesterday re-gluing the stands with a stronger hide glue.

I pushed open the barn door, pausing as my eyes adjusted to the pitch black interior. And also, if I was being honest, because it was hard wanting to step into said pitch black interior after the spooky creak the door made. It was as if I'd spent all night listening to some record of "Haunting Sounds for Haunted Houses," like the sound effects discs they used to produce for radio plays. I pulled my jacket tighter around me, shoving the bottles of glaze into my pockets so I had a free hand to hold up my phone's flashlight.

Still, the barn was large enough that the phone's light hardly made a dent. Unfortunately, some genius contractor who-knows-how-long-ago decided to wire the building such that the main light switch was on the opposite wall from the door.

You know, like normal. I felt my way along the workbench that ran the perimeter of the room, gingerly stepping over piles of wood cutoffs and trying not to catch my sleeve on any tools that might be lying around. They were basically deadly weapons, after all, capable of slicing right through vintage wool. My clumsiness had quickly become apparent to Ryan, who tried to guide me towards safer hand tools in answer to my many questions, and subtly tried to suggest that I avoid power tools at all costs. Or at least, not without his assistance. I tried to ignore the dire look on his face as he made that particular proclamation. I had, actually, been trained in the woodshop at school, getting to write my name on the wall along with the other students who were now approved to use the power tools. But then, like any sensible person aware of how clumsy she is, I then proceeded to spend the next three years studiously avoiding the woodshop at all costs.

The flashlight landed on my stand experiments further down the bench and I propped the phone up, quickly examining each joint. So far, so good. It looked like everything would hold up okay.

As the wind blew the door loudly shut, I jumped, knocking my phone to the floor. I knelt to pick it up, blindly feeling around while desperately trying not to imagine the many things I might come across; a rusty nail seemed to be about as good as it would get. As my hand connected with my phone and I lifted it up, the light caught an odd object lying behind a freestanding workbench a few feet away. I froze, half crouching, as my barely-awake brain struggled to process what I was seeing.

I crept forward, no longer thinking about what I might come into contact with and certainly no longer planning the funny story I would tell about this later, until I could clearly see around the workbench. The beam of light shook as I took in what I was seeing: Eliot, lying on the ground. If the chisel sticking out of his chest was any indication, he was very much dead. I crawled closer, leaning forward with a trembling hand as I felt for a pulse. Definitely dead. I was already regretting my earlier thoughts about deadly weapons in the wood shop.

Well, I was certainly awake now. Suddenly, all I could think about was how odd it was that you could be both freezing cold and covered in sweat at the same time. My own heartbeat drowned out any other noises as I sized up the situation: I was standing in a creepy old barn with a dead body again. Actually, not again, I corrected myself, since the last time wasn't a barn.

But there was no time for equivocating now. I forced myself to walk calmly and not run to turn the lights on, as I dialed 911. Almost as scary was the thought of having to tell Arun, Steph and Rebecca that yes, I found a dead body. Again.

4

Chapter 4

By mid-morning, the sight of flashing red and blue lights across the front yard was already getting old. Aside from the few who preferred to wait inside where it was warm, most of us had been standing huddled at the yellow crime scene tape, in the freezing cold, for the better part of an hour, unable to tear ourselves away. Every ten minutes or so, one of us would say how we should really go in now, and everyone else would murmur in agreement and stay right where they were. Did I mention it was freezing?

The police had made quick work of roping off the woodshop, coming in and out in their white suits, looking as efficient as you could while wearing paper shoes over snow boots. Madeline had brought out thermoses of coffee for everyone, including the two uniformed officers who were currently standing on the other side of the yard, regarding us about as wearily as you would lions whose cage you had some structural concerns about.

I moved quietly to the back of the group, waiting for a crime scene tech to walk out of the barn, distracting everyone, then I slipped off as quickly as I could, ducking around the back of the farmhouse. Although I'd been told to wait where I was, it looked like everyone was still busy enough not to miss me for a quick smoke break. Plus, there was a phone call I had to make. And I wanted to get it over with sooner rather than later. I chugged the rest of my coffee for fortitude and then dialed.

"Morning, love, you're up early," Arun answered, sounding already awake and cheery. So cheery that, did I really have to tell him? It would only ruin what sounded like a great mood. Right? I took another long gulp of coffee, hoping fortitude was on its way.

"Don't tell Rebecca," I blurted out. And instantly regretted it. That was somehow even worse than saying, "I have bad news." But in my current nearly frostbitten, sleep addled state, I couldn't figure out a better way to ease into the story.

"What's wrong, Sam?" Arun replied sharply, instantly concerned in exactly the way I hadn't meant to cause. "I'm here with Steph," he added. I could hear her in the background, clanging dishes around. It was only eight a.m., and it sounded like I'd caught them at breakfast.

"Well, kind of a funny story," I started. I should maybe have thought this through a bit more before calling. "Or not. But unfortunately, one of the other artists was killed." I figured I could get to the whole stumbling-over-his-body thing at a later date.

"Oh, my god, Sam, I'm so sorry to hear that," Arun said. "What happened?"

"No one knows yet. The police are here now," I paused, wondering how much later that date could really be. "It was Eliot, that guy I was telling you about? He was found in the woodshop this morning."

"Do you think someone could have broken in and attacked him?" Arun asked.

"I wish," I said - without thinking it through. Doing great so far, Sam. In fairness, a stranger breaking in would have been the easiest, least complicated explanation. And maybe there was still hope for an interrupted burglary. "But it doesn't really look like that. I think he was killed with a chisel. Kind of an artistic weapon, you might say." You might, if you'd already decided it was definitely another artist and you were definitely going to have to figure it out for yourself. Because, if for no other reason, what did the police know about artists?

I swear I could hear Arun's jaw clenching over the phone. That strong, handsome jaw. Which I was currently aggravating.

"You have to be careful, Samantha," he warned. Arun had recently taken to using my full name when he wanted me to know that he really meant it, like whenever he was telling me to be careful about something. I'd noticed this habit the first time Arun had seen me driving.

"Really careful this time," he continued. "You're stuck in a house with ten other people, any one of whom could be a killer. Plus, I'm four hours away, at least," Arun sighed. "And that's before even more snow comes."

"I know, but — " I started.

"No, Samantha. Really. I don't want to get another call a few days from now that, god forbid, something's happened to you because you couldn't stay out of this." It seemed hard to argue with that. We were both quiet for a few moments, save for the sounds of Steph continuing to cook in the background. It was somehow reassuring to know that a little old murder hadn't interrupted her breakfast plans. I shifted on my feet, wishing I'd thought to grab boots instead of slippers, and listening to the crunch of snow while I reasoned out a reply.

"Well, what if something happens to me because I *don't* look into this?" I asked. "When did the police ever get to a killer sooner than I did?"

"Many times," Arun replied easily, "None of which you were involved with."

"You know what I mean. I just think…there's been a lot going on here. With the thefts and everything, and now Eliot's been killed. I've been here the whole time. If anyone is in a good position to figure this thing out, I think it'd be me."

"Samantha — " Arun was cut off as Steph stormed over, yanking the phone away.

"We all know you're going to get involved no matter what we say. You're loud enough to hear even without the speakerphone on," she said, answering my unspoken question. At least that saved me from having to go through everything twice.

"Just don't do anything too stupid. Make friends with the lead detective and make sure you actually call them if anything happens," Steph continued, laying out ground rules that I'm sure Arun would soon protest.

"And most importantly, you need a good ally there. How many times have we saved your ass?" We all agreed it had been a few times. "So find someone you can trust. And stick with them," Steph said, handing the phone back to Arun without waiting for my reply.

"Should I just come up there now?" Arun asked. I could see him mentally going through his work calendar, playing an impossible game of tetris to try and rearrange things.

"No, honey, of course not. It's going to be fine and I know you can't get away from work right now," I replied. Plus, judging from the threatening gray clouds currently rolling in, Arun might have been right about more snow coming.

"I promise I'll be careful. When have I not?" I rushed on before anyone could answer that. "It's a small group of people. The odds are in my favor that it'll be easy to figure out which one of us killed someone yesterday." Pretty sure that's how chance and odds work, anyway. I heard the crunch of approaching footsteps coming around the side of the house. Official sounding footsteps.

"Listen, I have to go now but I'll call you later. Promise. Love you," I signed off. I guess that could have gone worse. I reviewed my mental list of Steph's ground rules, swearing I'd actually listen to her this time.

"Samantha Green?" A deep voice called, as one of the uniformed officers peered around the back of the house. "Detective Peters is ready to see you."

*

"So tell me one more time. Why were you in the woodshop at six this morning?" Detective Peters sat back, pinching the bridge of his nose, eyes shut. If I was right about anything, it was that the police had little patience for us artists.

"I'd left some work in the woodshop last night," I said again, trying to keep my voice slow and calm, without sounding like I was trying to speak down to anyone. Was it worse to actually be a pretentious artist, or to fall over yourself trying to prove you weren't one? Plus, there was the - in my opinion completely fair - frustration of having already been through this twice. "I woke up early and couldn't get back to sleep, so I decided to come to the studios and went in to get my work from the woodshop first."

Detective Peters sat forward again, trying to get comfortable on the rickety painting stool. They had commandeered the studio building for this initial interview and it seemed like it was a distracting, and downright uncomfortable, setting for at least one of us. In fairness, those stools are pretty uncomfortable for anyone, especially if you happen to be over six feet and, like Detective Peters, have no idea what to do with such long legs while balancing precariously.

"And you didn't see anyone else? Coming out of the woodshop, or any of the other buildings?" I'd racked my brain the first time he'd asked this question and still thought the answer was no. I gave an involuntary shiver as I imagined that someone had been creeping about in all the shadows that morning.

"No, I didn't see anyone. I'm not sure if anyone else was awake, though," I added helpfully. Or I hoped it was helpful. "I didn't hear anyone else moving around in the house this morning, but other people might have been up already."

"What about yesterday?" Peters asked. "What were you doing from about five o'clock on?"

"I worked in the woodshop, on those stands I mentioned, until about five thirty. Then I came over to the pottery shed and worked there until about seven. Maybe a little after?" I paused to wonder how the detective was keeping track of these details, without a notebook in sight. I inadvertently smiled at the memory of how Detective O'Connor, another police detective I'd met on a number of occasions, always made such a show of snapping his little notebook open and shut. As if it contained all the secrets of the world.

"Something funny, Samantha?" Detective Peters asked, eyebrows raised.

"No, no. Sorry. And it's just Sam, by the way," I said, regaining my composure. What was it about detectives that could put you on edge and send you into nervous giggles? Oh, right. Probably the murder and the crime and all that.

"After the pottery shed, I came back to the farmhouse and had a quick dinner before going up to my room. Everyone else had already eaten, so I was the only one in the dining room," I added, anticipating his next question. "I heard a few televisions on and some music, but didn't see anyone else the rest of the night. I hung out in my room until just past eight, when I went outside to smoke and call my friend Stephanie."

"See anyone else outside? Anyone coming or going?" Peters asked.

"Not really," I shook my head. "Timothy came up to borrow a lighter just before eight, and I saw him go back inside the house a few minutes later. I only noticed cause I was waiting for some privacy to call Steph."

"Why did you need so much privacy that you had to go outside, alone, to make a phone call?" Peters looked at me with a searching gaze that I was pretty sure they taught one just like it to detectives in Interviewing Potential Suspects 101. Wherever he'd learned it, it was effective.

"Oh, you know. It's like making a phone call when the subway's crowded. The walls upstairs are paper thin," I said. "It's a pretty old house. Seventeen hundreds, I think?" Peters was silent, waiting. I guess he wasn't looking for architectural details.

"Look, people are snarky. They gossip. Even in small groups like this where we've only just met each other. I just wanted to be able to talk without worrying about every tiny thing I said. Honestly, in the end, we mostly talked about Steph's parents." Steph had recently gone back to nursing school after a couple of years hiatus. Her parents were beyond thrilled but her mom, Sita, had instantly moved on to her next worry: When was Steph going to get married? It sounded tense, but I was only happy Sita wasn't badgering Arun with the same question. Although, it did once prompt me to surreptitiously google "traditional Cambodian wedding," and I had to admit, it looked pretty spectacular.

Detective Peters was nodding slowly, still silent. I stayed silent, too, hoping but doubting that I'd be able to outlast him and not be the first to speak. I'm pretty sure I once heard that nervous suspects always give away too much. Or was that in a novel? Either way, I had to bite my lip to keep from talking - then realized that might make me look even more suspicious.

"Alright, so to summarize," Peters finally spoke, his voice calm and quiet but still managing to echo in the open studio space. "You worked all afternoon yesterday until you got back to the house around seven. You didn't see anyone else coming in or out of the house or other studio buildings late last night. This morning, you couldn't sleep," he paused here, making it clear how suspicious this sounded, as if every criminal was just an insomniac with nothing better to do. "So you came out to the woodshop to pick something up." That something was my work, but I didn't bother to cut in.

"And you found Eliot, lying behind a workbench, apparently killed with a chisel. Is that all correct?" Peters paused while I nodded to confirm. I had to admit, it didn't sound great for me: I didn't see anyone and I was working alone most of the day. I doubted a private phone conversation would give me much of an alibi.

"What about anyone else, strangers? Did you see anyone around yesterday who was new, any visitors?" Peters asked, not for the first time. I once again said that no, I hadn't seen anyone except the mailman. As loathsome as Eliot could be, I doubted even he would be able to make an enemy of the mailman that quickly.

"When you found Eliot this morning, did you touch anything?" Peters asked. I had a mental image of my hands, shaking, reaching to check Eliot's pulse.

"Only to check his pulse," I confirmed. Which was true, although I'd certainly had the strong urge to also check his pockets, but I'd thought better of it just in time. It was a shame, in a way, as he'd been wearing overalls - so many pockets just begging to be searched. I cleared my throat, trying to look collected. I could only hope that Peters hadn't somehow learned mind reading, too.

Detective Peters nodded, standing up. "Okay, I think we're done here, then. For now," he added. "We'll be coming back tomorrow to take more detailed statements from everyone." His tone was still calm, so I wasn't sure how much that was meant to be a warning. But if I had to guess, I would say it was definitely very much a warning.

"If you could please go into the house now, to the living room, that would be appreciated. We're asking everyone to gather there." I nodded, trying to walk calmly out of the studios as I wondered what kind of announcement the police had in store.

5

Chapter 5

This was definitely not a situation where I enjoyed being the last to arrive. Every head turned towards me as I entered the living room, even the uniformed officer at the door who stepped aside to let me in. I tried to slip quietly into an armchair next to Tony, but promptly tripped over the coffee table as I went. Of course.

Righting a luckily empty mug, I sat down, vaguely offering the room a tight-lipped smile. Next to me, Tony was regarding me with an even stare, not even trying to hide her study of me. Around the room, people stared alternately into the fireplace or at their own shoes. I reasoned that this was probably down to the fact that police had collected our phones during the interviews and they had nothing else to look at, and not because everyone thought I was suspect number one and was trying not to stare.

We all jolted to attention as Detective Peters entered the room, every head whipping towards him and every back sitting up a little straighter. I was almost surprised that no one actually stood up and saluted. Although it looked like Simon came close.

"Right," Peters started, pushing up his thin wire-frame glasses. The glasses were so small and trendy I'd wanted to comment on them during my interview, then thought better of it. What obnoxious thing was I going to say? My, Detective, those glasses look much too design-y for someone in northern Vermont. Although something told me that this young Black police officer may not be from around here originally.

"Thank you all for waiting here and for your patience this morning. I know this can't be easy. I'm sorry for your loss." As Peters spoke, he looked around the room, staring calmly at each of us in turn. I tried to smile when his gaze landed on me, then switched to a grimace in case he thought a smile was too cheeky. Falling somewhere between a smile and an exaggerated frown, I probably just looked demented. So far, I think that was two strikes against me. At least two.

"I appreciate that everyone already took the time to speak with us today, but my officers and I will be returning tomorrow to take more detailed statements from you all." Brandon looked ready to protest at this continued intrusion, then thought better of it as Evan shot him a warning look.

"We'll want to know anything and everything you can tell us about Eliot," Peters said. "What he was like, his life back home, what he did. Even what kind of artwork he made." I swear I could almost hear the air quotes about "artwork," but chose to ignore this. As Steph said, I would have to make friends with this Detective if I wanted to get anywhere. Especially if I was to get anywhere safely.

"Please take the rest of the day to think back on the past week that you've been here. Anything you can remember, even if it seems only remotely related to Eliot, could be helpful," Peters continued. "And remember, there's no such thing as tattling on each other here. This is a murder investigation." He let that sink in for a few moments as we sat silently. The fire crackled so loudly I almost jumped.

"That'll be all for today. Everyone has my card if you think of anything that can't wait for tomorrow," Peters said and turned to go, taking a few steps into the hallway before turning back. "Oh, and no one is leaving here until we apprehend whoever did this."

Brandon was practically on his feet, but Peters held up a hand in warning.

"That's a basic precaution," he said. "Obviously, we can't have a potential murder suspect leaving town. So for now, you can go into town as needed to get supplies. But no one is leaving the property and returning home for the time being." The hand stayed up as a collective grumble went around the room. "There'll be a police presence at the front gate here. You'll need to tell them where you're going when you leave. And believe me, they will notice if you don't return."

"This is completely unfair. You can't keep us here like this,"

Brandon protested, refusing to remain silent any longer. "We have rights, you know." Heads were nodding throughout the room, even as Evan was tugging on Brandon's arm, trying to get him to sit back down.

"This is the worst," he grumbled, shrugging Evan off but sitting back down nonetheless.

Peters looked like he was actually considering this. "Well," he said slowly, voice still calm despite the protests, "I should think the real worst is probably being killed in a remote woodshop." With that, Peters didn't stick around to hear any more complaints. We waited until the sound of heavy boots moving down the hallway grew faint, punctuated by the close of the front door.

"This is completely ridiculous," Brandon said, still pouting.

"Seems totally reasonable to me," Jenny replied. "Isn't that what they always say? Don't leave town?"

"Sure, but obviously none of us did this. Some crazy person must have broken in, some stranger. And now we're being punished." I may not have wanted to be stuck here, but I thought there may be one or two holes in Brandon's logic.

"Look, I'm sure the police will catch whoever did this quickly," Evan said, looking as if he was trying to reassure himself as much as Brandon. "Besides, it's not like they're keeping us in our rooms the whole time. We were going to be here for another couple of weeks anyway."

"I know, but it's just the principle of the thing." Brandon folded his arms across his chest.

"Actually, it seems like the principle of the thing is, someone killed someone and the police have to find out who it was." Jenny stood, surveying us. "Because until then, we're stuck here with a murderer."

*

Perhaps because of the wonderful mood that Jenny's comment had left us all in, dinner was so far quiet that night, save for the clink of silverware and the continued crackle of the fire in the next room. Even I was feeling a bit desperate at the prospect of being stuck here for who knows how long. Although I did think there was a certain kind of poetic justice to it: an artist, doomed to spend an eternity in an artists' residency program. The novel practically wrote itself.

"Alright, I'm just going to say it," Brandon said, breaking the silence so abruptly I saw Rachel jump. I waited with bated breath to hear what 'it' could possibly be. The soup was a bit bland tonight?

"I'm sorry that he died, but it's not like anyone here really loved Eliot," Brandon said, once he was sure he had everyone's attention. "Plus, I've heard this isn't exactly the first time he's gotten into trouble at a residency program." Evan kicked him under the table as he spoke, first discreetly, then with an added elbow when he didn't get the hint.

"What?" Brandon asked, wide-eyed. "I'm just saying. I've heard some stuff." Brandon shrugged, his nonchalant expression practically begging us to ask for more info. Next to me, Tony was rolling her eyes.

"What do you mean, stuff?" Jenny asked, taking the bait - surprisingly, since I'd thought her skin was a bit tougher than that, but then I guess murder affects us all in our own ways.

"Well," Brandon replied, setting down his silverware and settling in for the hot gossip he'd clearly been dying to tell us all afternoon. Even I had to smile: his expression was like a little kid on Christmas morning, unwrapping one secret after the next, prettying each one up with a big bow of innuendo.

"I heard that Eliot almost didn't get into the artist residency program at the L.A. Museum of Art because of certain rumors. Rumors of plagiarism." Brandon picked his spoon back up and pretended to busy himself with his meal again, while clearly waiting for more questions to come in.

"Oh, Brandon," Tony said with another eyeroll. "Just tell us the whole story."

"Or as much of it as you actually know," Jenny added.

"Well, my friend Carla was a program assistant there, so I heard this whole saga firsthand," Brandon replied. Oh, well, if he heard it from Carla, then it must be true.

"Apparently," Brandon continued, "Eliot had applied and been in the top running for last year's program. But then, the selection committee found out that — maybe, of course, this was just an accusation, but I mean, I, for one, am sure it's true — he copied several of the works in his portfolio."

"How did the committee find out?" Simon asked.

"Another artist complained, after a list of front runners was leaked," Rachel cut in. "It was actually a friend of mine." She continued eating, only to look up and see nine inquisitive faces looking back at her. Well, eight inquisitive faces and one pouting face, as Brandon was clearly unhappy at being usurped.

"My friend was the person who complained, not the one who was plagiarized," Rachel continued. "I don't know whose work was copied. We only heard rumors." Brandon, begrudgingly, had to admit that he didn't know the plagiarized artist either.

"So then what happened?" Jenny asked. "I mean, after the committee found out."

Brandon shrugged. "From the way Carla told it, they hemmed and hawed for a while, but ultimately decided they couldn't find enough 'hard proof' to verify either way that Eliot had copied anything. So they just let him in."

Jenny shook her head indignantly. "How could they do that? Who was on this committee, anyway?" she demanded.

"But I don't see what any of that has to do with this," Evan said.

"I'm only saying, Eliot didn't exactly have a great track record with programs like this," Brandon said, only to receive another kick, courtesy of Evan.

"I thought that you were convinced it was some random stranger?" Timothy asked.

"Sure, it probably was," Brandon said, suddenly the picture of reason again. "But if it wasn't, I have a feeling that there were plenty of people who, let's say, won't be shedding too many tears for Eliot." Brandon may not qualify as a Stephanie-approved trusted ally, but I had to admit, he was probably my best source of info so far. Or maybe ammo was a better word for this type of information.

"But how could someone Eliot knew have gotten here, broken in, and killed him, and then gotten out again without ever being seen?" Rachel asked. "Plus, what did they do? Fly here from L.A. with some kind of weapon?"

At that moment, I realized that the police must have withheld certain details from everyone. Certain chisel-related details, maybe.

"I heard it was a chisel," Simon said, innocently enough. Okay, maybe they didn't. He studiously avoided looking at Ryan, our lone woodworker, while delicately blowing on a spoonful of soup. I almost wanted to applaud the performances everyone was putting on tonight.

Down the table from me, poor Ryan was turning bright red.

I mean, I guess I probably shouldn't say "poor" Ryan yet. You know, without first proving that he hadn't really killed someone. But who kills someone with a weapon that so obviously belongs to them? Unless...

My train of thought was broken as I looked up and realized that everyone was staring at me. I looked around the table, taking in the diverse array of glasses looking back at me. I'd never really noticed Rachel's rainbow colored frames before, or Tony's heart-shaped ones, but thought that now was probably not the time to mention it.

I took another bite while I stalled for time, running through a catalog of Agatha Christie books in my head. Poirot was always so careful about what information he did and didn't share with suspected murderers, but I doubted he — or rather, Christie — decided that on the spot.

"It was really dark this morning," I said, settling on evasion instead of outright lying. "I didn't get a good look."

"Oh, come on, Samantha," Brandon cajoled, "You obviously got a good enough look to see that he was dead."

"Maybe some people wouldn't want to stick around and study a dead body," Tony said pointedly. If only you knew, Tony. But I wasn't going to mention the whole pocket-searching impulse now.

"Whatever it was, I bet the police will tell us tomorrow." For someone whose sworn enemy two hours ago were the police who were keeping him here, Brandon now looked downright gleeful at the prospect of their return.

"You know, the whole point of interviews is for *them* to get information out of *you*, not the other way around," Jenny said.

"I know, but it doesn't mean I can't try," Brandon replied. "Don't you all want to know what happened?"

"Of course, but I don't think the police are coming here just to tell you who their prime suspects are," Evan said. Brandon shot him a wounded look: et tu, Evan?

"Who do you think the suspects are?" Jenny asked. Just as I was starting to think she was a good candidate for an ally in all this, I realized that Jenny might enjoy stirring things up a bit too much to pass muster with Steph.

"Anyone who knew Eliot before this, of course," Brandon said. "Which is pretty much everyone here from LA, I'd think. Plus, obviously, whoever the chisel belonged to."

"Okay, enough." Rachel put her silverware down loudly. "Can we just finish the rest of this meal in peace? I think there's been more than enough talk of suspects and murder weapons. No one is enjoying this." Her tone was enough to mollify everyone, and soon only the sounds of eating and crackling fire remained. Although if you could be quiet at someone, I think Brandon's expression definitely qualified.

But Rachel was right about one thing: I was not enjoying this.

There were so many details, big and small, swimming around my head right now: plagiarism, chisels, dark mornings, Los Angeles. The only thing I knew for certain was, if I ever wanted to get out of here, I would have to figure out what happened to Eliot.

6

Chapter 6

The morning after the police left, the air was distinctly different in the house. Quiet now felt spooky. Old was starting to feel haunted, no longer refined and elegant. What had felt like a cozy getaway, a place you were lucky to find, now felt like, well. A crime scene. Everyone was on edge. I think we all expected Eliot to pop up suddenly, maybe out from behind the couch or up from the basement, as if this was some bad practical joke he'd decided to play. I could almost see everyone's hair stand on end as we listened to the creaking steps of someone else coming down to breakfast. It was almost a relief when the police arrived and immediately called me in for an interview.

Almost, of course, because now I was sitting in the studio building once again, being interviewed by Detective Peters. This morning, he'd been joined by a young woman police officer who'd introduced herself as Officer **Mallory**. I was just glad to see that at least one of them had a notebook today, even if, after ten minutes, I still couldn't tell if Officer Mallory was here to be the good cop to Peters' bad cop, or if they were doing neutral, unimpressed cop and neutral, unimpressed cop.

"So, Sam," Peters said, stretching his legs out. He'd had the forethought today to have a real chair brought in. "Tell me about Eliot."

"Well, I didn't know him before I got here last week, so I don't really know how much there is for me to tell you," I replied, trying to stretch my own legs out. Unfortunately, they hadn't brought real chairs in for all three of us so I was perched on a rickety painting stool, trying to stretch out - while narrowly avoiding a large green stain that I hoped wasn't wet.

"First impressions are important. You probably learned a lot about him this past week," Peters said, staring at me expectantly. I scooted to the left a bit, trying to get the glare reflected in his glasses just right, to block his impassive stare.

"I guess. To be honest, my first impression was that Eliot was not a particularly nice person," I said. What did I have to lose by being honest? Except that out of everyone in the room, only I knew that I hadn't done it. I glanced down at the paint-covered stool: maybe it was all a ploy to keep your main suspect uncomfortable?

"But I never had any problem with him, personally," I added. "Eliot was always perfectly polite to me."

"But he wasn't to everyone?" Peters raised his eyebrows.

"I mean, I don't know if I'd say he was impolite, exactly." Except that's exactly what I just said. Before I walked in, I'd promised myself I'd keep the dithering to a minimum. Great job so far, Sam.

"It's just that, Eliot could be kind of mean sometimes. Nasty - but about little things," I said. "Like, he was critical of the brand of paints that Brandon uses. Or one time, I saw him tease Jenny about some top she was wearing. Stupid stuff, really." Peters nodded as if I had just said the most insightful thing anyone's ever said.

"Nothing bigger than that? Did anyone ever get into fights with Eliot? Even over little things?" Peters asked.

"Not that I ever saw," I replied, truthfully.

"Just between us," Detective Mallory cut in, "What was the gossip about Eliot like? Did you hear about any fights, or anything like that?" She leaned in, like we were just two girls having a chat. So I guess they were doing good cop and neutral, unimpressed cop.

"I don't think there really was any gossip about Eliot, to be honest. Or if there was, I certainly didn't hear it," I added. At least part of that was true: I was sure there had definitely been some kind of gossip about Eliot. His whole personality practically begged for people to talk about him behind his back. But I wasn't lying when I said I hadn't heard any of said gossip myself. Not a lot of any kind gossiping happened when I was alone in the pottery shed, where I had been for most of the week.

"Okay," Peters said, shifting his weight as if to signal a change in tactic. "Let's talk about the other artists here. What's been your impressions so far? Who've you made friends with, who's bothersome? That kind of thing." I couldn't remember the last time I heard anyone described as "bothersome," but I had a feeling I might not be the only one here who spent a lot of time reading old British mystery books.

"Honestly, I haven't given it much thought," I said, somewhat truthfully. The previous night, after the moderate train wreck of dinner, I'd lain awake going through each artist in turn, considering everyone as a more or less viable suspect until I fell asleep, like counting criminal sheep. I woke up to a mess of autocorrected notes on my phone, none of which made any particular sense. Unless "Evan paint duck" was some kind of stunning insight. So much for my brilliant detective mind.

"I'm really just here to work, not to make friends," I added, aware that I sounded like every contestant on a reality TV show ever. Which, as a side note, this was probably a great idea for a reality show. Just the artist residency part, that is, not the murder part. Although I guess it did give the setting a kind of *Survivor* edge.

Mallory made a note in her book, scribbling away for far longer than I seemed to actually talk.

"Come on, Sam, I'm sure you thought about the other artists," Peter said. "What about Ryan?" He asked so casually, it made it sound like this thought had only just occurred to him. But given the chisel I had seen the previous morning, that couldn't possibly be true.

"What about Ryan?" I replied. "He seems perfectly nice to me. He'd helped me with the stands that I was working on the other day, and with using some of the other tools in the woodshop."

"Did you ever see him and Eliot have any kind of disagreement?" Peters asked. "Or did Ryan ever say anything to you about him?"

"I don't think Ryan ever said anything to me about anyone, period," I said. Peters nodded, silently waiting for me to go on.

"You guys don't actually think that Ryan did this, do you?" I looked back and forth between the two detective's faces. Mallory looked slightly surprised, but Peters' expression was unchanged. "If you were going to kill someone, would you really do it with a murder weapon that immediately pointed to you?"

"I don't know, Sam, I can't say that I've given a lot of thought to how I would kill someone," Peters replied evenly. "What about you?"

Okay, so I might have painted myself into a corner on that one (no art pun intended).

"No, of course I haven't thought about how I would kill someone," I said. "All I'm saying is, Ryan is just the most obvious suspect, because of the weapon. But only because of the weapon. That doesn't mean anything."

"Not necessarily, no," Peters said, looking at me thoughtfully. I wasn't sure I wanted to be in his thoughts quite that much. I quickly tried to remember what the top ten results had been the last time I googled myself, imagining what Peters' was about to find given that, judging from his look, looking me up would definitely be his next step. I could only hope that some press release about the graduating seniors exhibit would trump any remaining articles about the one or two dead bodies I may have been linked to in the past. I mean, definitely linked to.

"Well, thank you, Sam. You've given us a lot to think about this morning," Peters said, crossing his arms as he continued to gaze at me from behind those wire-rim glasses. With that, it seemed, I was dismissed.

*

I fled through the icy yard to the pottery shed. Although the woodshop was still closed and the studio building otherwise occupied, the pottery shed was mercifully empty. I stood in the doorway, gulping in the cool air and the comforting smell of damp clay. I kept trying to tell myself that I had nothing to worry about but somehow, the idea that I was a suspect in a police investigation was more worrying than the idea that I had a killer to catch.

I sat down at the wheel, not even bothering to take off my jacket, just pushing my sleeves up. I peeled back the plastic from around a chunk of clay, slicing off a piece and beginning to center it on the wheel. Despite the comforting motions of shaping the spinning clay, I couldn't lose myself in the rhythms of the pottery wheel as I normally did. After about twenty minutes, and more than one failed attempt to shape a form that wasn't lopsided, crooked, or about to fall over, I gave up.

I stood, figuring there were worse ways to spend a day than hunkered down in bed with a good book, if I could find one that was distracting enough, but I paused in the doorway. From the entrance of the pottery shed, I realized I had a clear view across the yard to the studio building. Which meant I could see the other artists coming and going from their respective interviews. Which meant I could, albeit at a slight distance, gauge everyone's reactions before and after being questioned about a murder that one of us had committed. What that would tell me, I wasn't sure, but it suddenly seemed like a much, much better idea than going inside and reading.

Putting practically all my body weight behind it, I pushed the table with the pottery wheel over towards the door, angling it so I'd have a clear view of the studio building but was still in a position to at least look like I was focused on working. After me, Ryan had been called and was still in there now. I checked the time on my phone, groaning slightly at the idea of being questioned by Peters for almost thirty minutes.

I busied myself with setting up another piece of clay, not even bothering this time to really center it properly. I kept my eyes glued to the wheel until I heard the door to the studio building creak open. I pretended to rinse my hands in the bucket of water I kept next to the wheel while I watched Ryan exit. Ramps had been installed at the front doors to each of the buildings for Tony, and Ryan's plodding steps down it now seemed to give new meaning to the phrase "walking the plank." The poor guy looked utterly miserable, like he'd just spent the previous hour being questioned from all angles about a murder in which he was the number one suspect. I knew I shouldn't be so sympathetic without finding at least a little evidence first, but Ryan just didn't strike me as a likely suspect. No one with the amount of patience it takes to watch me use a table saw has the kind of temper that would suggest routine bouts of murderous rage.

Ryan barely looked up as Brandon walked by, on his way to his own interview, accompanied by a uniformed officer keeping a judicious distance. Judging from his jaunty swagger, it looked like this was all one big game to Brandon. I rolled my eyes, not bothering to study his face too closely as he crossed the last few feet to the studio building. What more could that expression tell me? Although, I reasoned, there was always the possibility it was all swagger, no substance, just one big ruse designed to mask actual feelings of suspicious nervousness. I wished that I had Stephanie or Rebecca here with me, anyone to give me a second opinion. This entire figure-out-who-killed-Eliot business suddenly seemed much harder to do solo. I made a mental note to prioritize Steph's rule about finding an ally.

Without realizing it, I let my focus go soft, like an old television with a slight snow of static, as I became absorbed in the clay in front of me. A bulbous vessel was taking shape when I jolted back to attention at the sound of footsteps clanking down the ramp across the yard. I looked up just in time to see Brandon's face as he headed back towards the farmhouse. His amused nonchalance had been entirely replaced by genuine concern: a worried, grim expression was on his face as he walked slowly through the yard, not even bothering to keep his suede sneakers on the path and out of the snow. Perhaps Detective Peters had brought home to him the reality of a murder investigation. Or maybe Brandon had more to worry about than meets the eye.

A uniformed officer had trailed Brandon back to the farmhouse, and was now crossing back to the studio building once more with Madeline Berry in tow. I was surprised to see her being called for an interview, then kicked myself for not thinking about her sooner. Of course, even if she wasn't an artist, she'd been here the whole time, too. Although I had no idea what reason a calm, middle-aged woman from Vermont had for killing a young artist from L.A. - especially one whom she'd only just met. But if I was going to go through everyone in the house, I would definitely have to include Madeline. She hadn't been particularly forthcoming so far, when we were all just meeting, which of course now made me wonder why not. All I knew for sure was that she was from Vermont originally and had worked at Winterbrook Residency for five years. I wondered if there was anyone around town who might be able to fill in some details for me. We'd only been into the town once, to go to a grocery store, but I'd noticed a coffee shop and a library on the small main street. I added "interrogate townspeople" to my mental list of tasks, smiling at the eyeroll I would have gotten from Steph for that.

Madeline's expression was remarkably unchanged as she left

the building soon after, her interview shorter than most. I wasn't sure if that was a sign of a clear conscience or extremely good acting. If this was a novel, I'd soon find out that she used to be an actress, hiding some dark past and probably a secret child or two. In reality, she probably just wanted to work close to home and needed a good job. I wondered if she'd known beforehand that this is how it would be working for artists. Madeline's gait was unhurried as she walked through the yard, giving a small wave as she passed Tony, the next victim.

"I should start by telling you it's medicinal," I heard Tony announce as she wheeled into the studio building, Peters opening the door for her. I stifled a laugh, but apparently not quickly enough. Peters was staring straight at me, perfectly still where he stood, holding the door open even after Tony had disappeared inside. I tried to turn my laugh into an extended cough, but I wasn't fooling anyone. I nearly snapped myself in two bending over the pottery wheel, trying to appear as absorbed as possible in my work. But it didn't look like Peters would be going anywhere until I left and I didn't particularly want to find out what would happen if I didn't. I quickly wiped my hands off, not even bothering to clean up the wheel before I fled the pottery shed.

*

I leaned against the back wall of the farmhouse, waiting for my heartbeat to slow down again. Detective Peters definitely had a knack for making you feel suspicious, even when you knew with absolute certainty that you'd done nothing wrong. It would be hard to follow Steph's instructions to make friends with him. I couldn't really imagine being Peters' friend, in any scenario. I shuddered at the thought, reaching for my cigarettes just as the farmhouse door creaked open.

"Just the girl I was looking for!" Jenny cried as she came out the back door and saw me standing there, hunched against the cold.

"Happy to see you too, but why me?" I asked, offering her a light. Jenny tossed both her long hair and over sized scarf over her shoulder, looking around dramatically as if we were about to act out a scene in which two suspects get their alibis straight.

"Well, I've been reading up about you," she said. "Obviously everyone looked each other up when we all got here," she added as she saw the expression on my face. Somewhere between confusion and amusement. Probably some fear mixed in there too, if I'm being honest. I can't say all the newspaper photos out there were of my most flattering side. I mean, I hoped I had a flattering side.

"Since it sounds like you're not exactly new to all this, I figured you'd be the perfect person to talk to," Jenny said, drawing a big circle with her cigarette to describe what all "this" was.

"Talk to about what, exactly?" I asked wearily.

"Eliot. The body. Suspects," Jenny said with relish. "Who do you think did it?"

Okay, so we were going right for it.

"Honestly, I have no idea yet," I replied. Jenny looked ready to protest, shooting me a disbelieving glare, and I rushed on. "But what did you think about all that plagiarism stuff last night? What Brandon was saying about the LA residency."

Jenny waved her hand dismissively. "That was all nonsense. It was just some story going around," she said. "I don't think there's really anything to it." She took a long drag, looking over her shoulder again as if there were spies everywhere. I couldn't help but smile.

"If you ask me, I think Brandon is a pretty likely candidate," Jenny said with a knowing nod. "He's been all over Evan since we got here, but Evan wasn't exactly immune to Eliot's charms."

"Do you really think he'd kill someone over a few days of jealousy?" I asked, while wondering what Eliot's charms had even been. If he'd had any, they certainly hadn't been on display for the rest of us, although, looking back now, I did remember seeing him and Evan together a few times, not exactly looking uncomfortable. The idea of Brandon acting in jealousy had honestly occurred to me, too, but I wasn't sure how much weight to give it.

"Oh, you know Brandon," Jenny said vaguely. "I wouldn't put it past him." We were both silent for a few moments, considering this.

"Okay, or, if it wasn't Brandon, I bet it was Ryan," Jenny said. "It's true, isn't it? About the chisel?"

I was silent for a beat too long.

"I knew it!" Jenny cried. "And he's the only one here who brought his own woodworking tools."

"But what motive would Ryan have?" I asked.

"Does that matter?" Jenny shrugged. I gave her my best side-eye.

"Yeah, I would say that matters a little," I replied. Hopefully it mattered a bit more to the police than it clearly did to Jenny.

"Well, what about the means?" Jenny leaned closer. "I heard him leave his room that night."

"What time?" I asked.

"About seven thirty. I remember because my podcast had just ended, so I heard it very clearly." I looked at the glee on her face and assumed it had been a true crime podcast.

"What did you hear, exactly?" I asked.

Jenny shrugged. "Ryan leaving his room. The door closing. You know, the sounds of someone coming in and out. He has the room across from mine, so I know it was him."

"Did you look out and see him?"

"No, but why would I have? It's not like I knew he was on his way to kill someone." Reasonable enough, but it meant that Jenny could have heard anyone. I said as much.

"Well, you know best!" Jenny said cheerily, crushing out her cigarette and turning to go. "Just keep me updated, 'kay?" I found myself nodding before I even realized what I was agreeing to.

It would've been funny if it wasn't so concerning. Clearly, people had already made up their minds and the popular opinion had picked Ryan as the best candidate for murderer. I knew there wasn't anything I could do, yet, to sway the opinion - or even if I should. For all I knew, Ryan was an evil genius who'd deliberately planned a murder in which he was such an obvious suspect that it seemed it couldn't possibly be him.

I sighed, shoving my hands into my pockets for warmth and once again regretting that I hadn't listened to Rebecca about packing more gloves. I shut my eyes at the thought of having to tell her about all this and wondered how long I could put it off. I knew Steph wouldn't go out of her way to mention it, but Rebecca went into the Phans' store all the time and was bound to find out, sooner or later. I just hoped it was later. Like, after it was all cleared up, later.

I owed Arun and Steph an update, and tapped out a quick message to Arun first: *Police here again today. Told them everything I know, basically nothing.* So far, so honest. *Lying low, no plans so far.* A little less honest. *Love you!* Definitely honest.

Knowing Steph would need less reassurance, I wrote a slightly different message for her: *You've been usurped. Detective Peters my new BFF.* Steph was quick to respond: *Great, didn't need you anyway.* I laughed, watching the three little dots as I awaited her next witticism. *I just hope you're being serious for once. Love you!!!*

Ordinarily, Steph's true sign of love would be a series of deeply sarcastic remarks. This seemed much worse, much more worrying, and I did, in fact, feel dead serious for once. I did intend to lie low, like I'd told Arun, but a plan had been forming in my mind as I'd listened to Jenny's suspicions. As much as I wanted to know more about the plagiarism story, it seemed like there was one thing at the center of all this. Or rather, a series of things: the missing objects. It wasn't that I'd deliberately not told Detective Peters about the thefts. He just hadn't asked. And in fairness, it hadn't been top of mind when I first found Eliot. But now, I had to ask myself: What are the chances that among ten artists were both a thief and a murderer? I paused, considering the other artists I knew. Okay, so actually it seemed like the chances might be fairly high. But I still couldn't imagine that two completely unrelated crimes had happened in the same week, among the same small group of people. And with only the one car here, it would've been difficult to get all the stolen items out of the house without anyone noticing. Which meant they must still be around here. Somewhere. I knew I couldn't find Eliot's killer just by looking around, but I might, just might, be able to find the missing objects.

It was a natural human impulse to look for the meaning in

patterns. Right? It's not that I was morbidly curious about things that other people would want no part of. Or should that be a question? I shook off that last thought as I stubbed out the cigarette, my resolve returning. It was definitely a pattern. And it was definitely natural to want to find out more.

7

Chapter 7

By breakfast the next morning, my resolve had wavered only slightly. If no one else had been able to find the objects, then why did I think I could? Still, when had that really stopped me before?

I'd spent the evening staring at a list of the stolen objects: heat gun, canvas, pigments, sketchbook. The canvas and pigments obviously went together, but the heat gun still seemed like an outlier to me. I was planning to call and ask Rebecca if one would ever be useful in painting, just as soon as I figured out some way to ask that without revealing everything else. I wasn't sure whether to consider the sketchbook an outlier, too. It wasn't exactly painting-related, but could still be used for materials, I guess. Plus, I still couldn't rule out the possibility that any one of these objects had just been mislaid, a kind of accidental red herring. Or even that more than one person here had been behind the thefts. I had a flashback to those trees we used to have to make in elementary school math classes, to figure out how many combinations it was possible to make with three or four things: *If there were nine artists and four objects missing, how many artists could have stolen each object?*

Everyone was quiet over breakfast, so far, just the usual hurried hush of sipping coffee and downing toast while checking our phones and scrolling through the latest news. It seemed like no one was really wide awake much before noon, so none of the other artists noticed that I was the last one left at the table. Pretending to be engrossed in a *New Yorker* review of some Chelsea gallery show I'd never go to, I waited until I heard the last footsteps head out, the door closing as everyone finally left for their respective studios.

In the quiet, I crept back up the staircase. I was pretty sure that Madeline was still working in the kitchen and I tried to shake off the feeling that at any moment, I'd turn around and she'd be right there, looking over my shoulder. I took a deep breath, trying to will my hands to stop shaking as I reached for the doorknob to Ryan's room. For all she - or anyone - knew, I was an absent minded artist, returning for something I forgot and walking into the wrong room, accidentally. That was believable, right? Hopefully I wouldn't have to find out.

I stepped into Ryan's room and quietly shut the door behind me, taking a moment to get my bearings. Since it was an old farmhouse, added onto over the years, each of the bedrooms was a bit different. Ryan's was smaller than mine, in a newer part of the house, and featured a large bay window looking out onto the yard. I ducked down, below the window, and reached up, fumbling to get the curtain drawn and rolling my eyes at my own ridiculousness. Everyone was hard at work.

Not standing around the yard, looking up into the windows to catch someone snooping around. I mean, investigating.

I stood back up, surveying his belongings. Ryan had unpacked neatly, just a few stacks of clothes in the dresser, a few assorted belongings on the nightstand, and two work bags in the corner. I made quick work of the clothes and nightstand, not finding anything out of the ordinary - except that Ryan apparently took prescription sleeping pills. I wondered if there was any way I could possibly find out when he usually took them, and if I could triangulate that to whenever Jenny heard - or thought she heard - him leaving. In any event, I had a feeling that Ryan had probably slept through the whole grisly scene.

I turned now to the tool bags, opening up the heavy canvas bags to reveal a mini woodshop inside. I took out files, sandpaper, every size of screwdriver, and hammers in shapes I didn't even know existed. And, at the bottom of the bag, a canvas roll holding five chisels, with an empty slot for chisel number six. I had a feeling I knew where that one might be now.

So Ryan kept his tools in his room, and brought them over to the woodshop each day. In fact, I'd seen him leaving that morning with a milk crate full of wood scraps, a canvas tool roll on top, identical to the one I was looking at now. On the one hand, it made it all the more likely that Ryan had simply forgotten a tool that day, and left one chisel lying around the wood shop, a perfect weapon of opportunity for our murderer. On the other hand, if Ryan was really clever, that's exactly what he would want people to think.

I looked up at the sound of laughter outside, peeking out the curtain to see Jenny and Brandon taking a break outside the studio building. I still had a couple of hours before anyone would come back for lunch, but knew I needed to get on with it, and quickly. I neatly replaced the tool bags in the corner and slowly opened the door, waiting until I was sure there was no one else upstairs before I left, and headed into the next room.

Unlike Ryan, it seemed like Rachel hadn't made much of an attempt to unpack neatly. There were clothes strewn all over the room, piled onto the bed and spilling out of the dresser, while the desk was stacked perilously high with books, papers, and miscellaneous art supplies. I picked my way through the mess over to the dresser, and methodically went through each drawer. Even if there was a possibility that I was currently searching a murderer's room, I still had to pause and admire the fact that a girl from California had somehow managed to bring more sweaters to a New England residency than I had.

Unfortunately, there was nothing of much note in the dresser, no easy clues left lying about for a currently clue-less detective to stumble upon. I made my way over to the desk, gingerly pushing aside a stack of painting books so I could sit down on the old wooden desk chair. I idly flipped through the stack (*Pictorial Textiles: 1700 to the Present; Flesh Made Cloth;* a monograph on Anni Albers) while casually leaning over and nudging the mouse pad of Rachel's laptop with my elbow. What? She's the one who left it asleep. And apparently without a password.

The laptop opened to about half a dozen open tabs, mostly art websites showing reviews and images of other artists' work. I didn't think there was anything particularly suspicious about reading a review of a new Jeff Koons sculpture, but filed that away for later. Who knows? Maybe it was indicative of a demented personality.

I clicked through to the last tab, scrolling through Rachel's inbox. There were a few emails about an upcoming show she was in back in L.A., amid a sea of newsletters and store promotions. I was tempted to forward myself an Artists and Craftsman Supply coupon, when I noticed an email with the subject line *HE'S HERE.* I clicked open the thread, which appeared to be four or five emails between Rachel and a friend of hers whose name - clearly from a work address - showed up only as New Street Gallery.

I let out a low whistle as I read through the emails. The first few had been brief, sent on the first day of the residency, but told me everything I needed to know:

*He's here!! That **** from the L.A. MFA residency.*
  The one who copied your work??
  Yes.

I stared at Rachel's simple "Yes," not even bothering to fully read her friend's indignant and lengthy reply. So Rachel had been very much lying when she said she didn't know who Eliot had plagiarized. He had plagiarized her, and now here he was at another residency program. Where he had since been killed. I may not have found any of the stolen objects yet, but this definitely seemed like a smoking gun.

I wasn't even sure where to start. If even Brandon hadn't known who Eliot plagiarized, then I didn't know who else could corroborate this story. And it made me wonder: Was Eliot even aware *this* Rachel was the one he'd plagiarized, or had she just been some nameless, faceless profile online, only good for source material? I had to assume this was the case. Or else Eliot was even more brazen and arrogant than I'd thought.

I took a quick picture of the laptop screen, then carefully turned it back to sleep mode and replaced the books as they had been on the chair. I did a quick sweep of the other items on the desk, mostly sewing implements and a few sculpture tools, including an impressive set of carving knives and a few knitting needles that now seemed far too sharp for their intended purpose. Although Eliot might have been killed by a chisel, I had no doubt that every one of us had at least one good murder weapon in our studio.

I was honestly pretty shaken by this discovery: the first real motive I'd found for Eliot's death, if you were a probably at least somewhat crazy artist who thought that plagiarism (at least where a prestigious residency was involved) was a good motive for murder. But I had a job to finish, and would have to put a pin in this for now.

I paused at the door, suddenly frantic at the sound of footsteps coming up the stairs, someone humming quietly. I looked around for somewhere to hide, silently cursing this old house and the tiny closets that even my five foot, two inch frame couldn't squeeze into. The footsteps passed Rachel's door and continued down the hall, and I risked a small peek out the door.

Madeline was efficiently restocking towels in the linen closet at the end of the hall and I breathed a (quiet) sigh of relief as she made her way back downstairs. I waited another moment before finally leaving, and ducking into the next room.

Even though they were only separated by one wall, Timothy and Rachel's rooms couldn't have been more different. Timothy's room was in an older part of the house, where the rooms still had dormers that neatly sliced each room in half diagonally. But I doubted that Timothy minded the small size: his room was practically monk-like, spare and nearly spartan. He'd filled only one drawer of the supplied dresser, a simple stack of flannel shirts and work pants. I scanned the rest of the room, which I could almost search without even moving. If Timothy had found a hiding place somewhere here, with nothing to hide behind, then he must have some serious sculpture skills.

Even though it was basically bare, I went over to the desk, double checking the drawers. There were a few papers, mostly plans for paintings and other works, and a few diagrams of what looked like frames. I paused as I brushed aside a couple papers, uncovering two small sketchbooks. I flipped through each, but they contained much the same as the loose papers: drawings, plans, a few supply lists. I wondered how many sketchbooks Timothy had brought, if there was a third one that was really stolen - or if he'd made the whole thing up. Although why he would, I had no idea. I made a mental note to ask him about the stolen sketchbook, wondering if he'd divulge whatever artistic secrets it probably held. I smiled as I pictured my own sketchbook, usually a mess of indecipherable scribbles and urgent, underlined reminders to MAIL RENT CHECK or

CALL MOM.

I must have been distracted by these thoughts, as I walked out of Timothy's room without stopping to make sure I was alone, and found myself a few steps into the hallway when I heard footsteps coming up the staircase. I froze. Jenny jogged up the stairs, bobbing to whatever tune was playing in her head. She looked up and thankfully didn't miss a beat as she saw me standing there, staring like a deer in headlights.

"Hi, Sam!" she called as she went into her room. "How's it going this morning?" She came out again, clutching an unopened bottle of turpentine that she now shook towards me.

"Just needed to come back for this," Jenny said. "Who knew how much turp you could go through in a week!" I returned her smile, hoping it looked normal and not, you know, like I had just been caught doing something I definitely shouldn't have been and now needed desperately to cover my tracks.

"Same here, actually," I said, patting the pocket of my flannel coat and hoping she wouldn't realize it was actually empty. "Somehow forgot my phone today." I tried not to look too relieved as Jenny didn't pause to question this, instead turning back down the stairs. I followed, making it out to the living room before stopping again.

"You know what? I should probably grab the charger. You go ahead without me," I said, waving her off. Jenny shrugged, blowing me a kiss as she walked off. I waited for the sound of the door closing before letting out the breath I'd been holding for that whole exchange.

The sounds of Madeline working in the kitchen just down the hall were a bit too close for comfort, especially now that I'd basically announced my presence. I ducked into the first doorway on my right, and found myself standing in Tony's room, the only one of us staying on the first floor.

Tony's room was spacious and bright, with airy white curtains letting in as much light as they could on a winter morning. She was not quite Timothy-level neat, but had certainly unpacked with care and I was extra cautious as I went through her clothes, careful not to be my usual careless self, flinging things around with abandon. Unfortunately, her dresser didn't reveal anything more interesting than the fact that she owned not one but two pairs of heart-shaped glasses.

I was replacing a stack of sweaters in the drawer when I heard the unmistakable sound of the door creaking open and Tony clearing her throat. I spun around, sweaters still in hand, as I desperately searched for something, anything, to say. A string of useless facts went through my head: the average life expectancy of a sea turtle, how old Georgia O'Keeffe was when she died, that Wee Gee was the first crime scene photographer. Okay, so all my facts were about death in one way or another, but I didn't have time to psychoanalyze that at the moment. Thankfully.

"I, uh...I like your glasses," I stammered. Great save, Sam. Tony shrugged, adjusting her frames as she wheeled herself into the room and closed the door behind her.

"It gives people something to stare at other than the chair," she said. "Now, what are you really doing here? Looking for the stolen stuff?" She appraised me calmly, a whole lot more calm than I felt right about then. Pretty sure my jaw was firmly on the floor, as words continued to desert me.

"It can't be the murder weapon, because obviously that was never lost. So it must be the thefts," she reasoned. "Find anything so far?"

So it was time to come clean. Fingers crossed that Tony was the Steph-approved ally I'd been looking for, and I wasn't about to spill the beans to a murderer.

"No, not really," I admitted. "A few things that are weird. Maybe suspicious. But none of the stolen stuff."

Tony nodded. "Yeah, that's what I would have thought. I have a feeling whoever stole the materials probably hid them just by using them, right? That would be the easiest. Hide them right in plain sight." I was simultaneously impressed and embarrassed that I hadn't realized that sooner. Clearly I wasn't the only one lying awake at night going over lists of stolen objects.

"Need any help?" Tony offered. She patted the armrest of her chair and added, "I may not be able to get upstairs and search everyone's rooms, but it's not like I can't talk to people, do some looking around the studios."

"Yes, please," I said with genuine relief. I took in her wry smile and matter-of-fact tone, and had a feeling that Steph would most definitely approve.

"Great, that's settled then. Let's meet up tomorrow to talk through everything," Tony said.

"We have to get away from here, though. Nowhere here is really private enough," I said. "Although…" I faltered.

"I can get in the van, Sam," Tony said, smiling at me benignly like I was a child. "Don't worry about it." She turned around to go and I stammered out an apology after her.

"It's cool, I've heard a lot worse." Tony turned to grin at me over her shoulder. "Oh, and you can put those sweaters back in the second drawer."

I looked down, realizing I was still clutching a stack of her clothes. Yep, I definitely thought Steph would approve. Anyone who could come in, realize you were searching their stuff for stolen items, and wind up teaming up with you to investigate? A solid ally if there ever was one.

*

I managed to search the remaining rooms before everyone started to trickle back for lunch, although my efforts revealed nothing more interesting than the fact that Simon was somehow still reading his way through *Harry Potter*, and Evan had brought a number of outfits that I doubted were suitable for a Vermont winter. If Tony was right, and the stolen materials had already been used, then I stood little chance of finding them. At least not in someone's room.

I pondered this as I spent the afternoon in the pottery shed, working my way through another batch of raku-fired vessels. Wearing the kind of long, leather gloves that you might use to handle a falcon, I reached into the kiln with a pair of tongs that were a few inches shorter than I'd have preferred for, you know, reaching into an oven that was about two thousand degrees hot. As I drew them out, I quickly plunged each vessel into a box filled with the dried leaves, twigs, and desiccated seed pods that I'd collected on my walks, watching as the materials instantly burned in the intense heat, leaving unpredictable swirls of charcoal on the clay. It was mesmerizing. Although it may have seemed hot in human terms, raku is actually a pretty low temp process as far as clay is concerned. At these temperatures, I knew the clay had gone through a process called sintering, with particles adhering to one another permanently, though it was still technically porous, as the clay wasn't getting hot enough for glass to form. Yep, I was a huge nerd and could talk mud all day.

But today, I knew there were bigger things I had to consider. I sighed, removing the heavy gloves after lifting the final pot out of the box and sitting down. I still hadn't figured out how I could ask Rebecca about the heat gun and painting without a plausible story, but the list of items would continue nagging at me until I could see with any finality exactly which items were related to each other, and how. I took out my phone and dialed before I could think twice.

"Hello?" Rebecca answered on the second ring. I could hear

a TV on in the background and assumed that, like a normal person, she was home after work at five o'clock and probably hanging out with Mel, our other roommate - instead of sitting in an old shed in some remote corner of Vermont, trying to find a murderer.

"Sam? How's everything going?" she asked, shushing Mel in the background.

"Good, good. Just had a quick question for you," I said, gearing up to ask about the stolen heat gun.

"Is this going to be about the guy who was killed?" she asked. "Because I saw Stephanie at their store. Someone forgot to get food for Paul so I had to go out last night. She told me everything." I could practically hear her glare at Mel, presumably the one who'd forgotten to feed our cat, and was thankful that this slight was somehow on par with my being involved in yet another murder investigation.

"Sorry I didn't tell you sooner," I said. "I just didn't want to worry you."

"You mean, you didn't want me telling you off for getting involved," Rebecca correctly guessed. "Whatever, Sam, I'm sure you already are. You know we all just want you to stay safe."

"I know, I know. I'm sorry," I replied, hoping we could fast-forward through the guilt trip. "I did just have one question: Is there ever a time that you would use a heat gun while painting?"

"A heat gun? I don't think so," she said slowly. "Maybe to help stretch fabric, if you were painting on something other than canvas? Or to dry out paint faster?" Her first guess was, in fact, what Rachel had used the heat gun for, to stretch out sized fabric - but that wasn't something I thought anyone else here would have had much use for.

"That's kind of what I thought," I confirmed. "But if you think of anything else, let me know."

"What's all this about, Sam?" Rebecca demanded. "What does a heat gun have to do with someone getting killed?" I heard Mel say something indistinct in the background. She was probably chomping at the bit to hear all the juicy details.

"Honestly, I wish I could tell you," I said with a sigh. "It's all still a bit of a mess at the moment." I gave Rebecca a rundown of the thefts and the lead up to Eliot's death.

"So you think maybe Eliot found out who the thief was? And they killed him to cover it up?" Rebecca asked.

"I guess that's a possibility," I replied. "But I don't think a few bottles of pigment are really worth killing over."

"No, probably not," Rebecca agreed. "Unless you thought the police would get involved. Or you reacted in the moment."

"True," I agreed, mentally flipping through my list of artists and wondering who had the kind of temper to react in the moment like that. "I honestly just don't know yet. I don't think I will until I can find even a sign of anything that was stolen."

"Sam, just be careful," Rebecca said. *"Mel, move over,"* I heard her hiss to the side, and laughed, knowing Mel would now demand a nightly news update until this was all over. If it was ever over. I stifled a groan, tamping down on the dread at being effectively trapped here until we knew what was going on. I took a deep breath and made my voice as cheery as possible, signing off with Rebecca.

So, the heat gun was probably not used by a painter, or at least not by a painter who used the most common techniques. If only that information actually got me anywhere. I stared at the row of vessels and blobby forms lining the shelves in the room, the swirling, muddy charcoal a fitting metaphor for my day.

8

Chapter 8

The next morning, Tony and I arranged to check the van out and made our way to the small coffee shop in town for brunch, and a debrief on my search for the stolen objects. Tony cemented her status as Steph-approved when she didn't even bother to critique my driving, just rolling her eyes silently at my only-slightly-botched parking job.

Settling in at a table in the corner of the cafe, Tony didn't waste any time getting down to business.

"My money's on Simon," Tony said, blowing a new pattern into her cappuccino. "The guy's so uptight. When people like that snap, it's always extreme." I had to admire how matter of factly she was talking, as if it were an everyday occurrence to find yourself sitting in a coffee shop, talking about a recent murder with someone you just met a week ago.

"You also shouldn't rule me out completely," Tony said, as she tore her blueberry muffin neatly in two. "In the interest of fairness," she said around a mouthful of berries. Tony looked up and saw my skeptical expression.

"What, you think that just because I use a wheelchair, I couldn't kill someone?" she shrugged, as we both pictured the height of the chisel we saw sticking out of Eliot, who, judging from the way he towered over me, had to be at least five eleven or twelve. "I'm just saying, I think we have to treat everyone as a suspect, until we definitely know otherwise. I was immediately suspicious of you," Tony said, pointing at me with the rest of the muffin. "I mean, the first person to find the body? Come on. Suspect number one, right there. But then I did a little reading up on you and it turns out, this is just weirdly something you do," she said, gesturing to the notes I'd laid out on the table to make it clear what "this" was.

"Well, assuming it wasn't either one of us, who else do you think is a suspect?" I asked, following her lead and forgoing any preamble. "Personally, I think it's a tough call. It's harder to think of anyone here who actually liked Eliot."

Tony nodded. "Definitely. Did you see the way Brandon had been looking at him? Like a cat getting fed up with a mouse for not being fun enough." I snorted out a laugh, trying not to choke on my coffee. It was definitely the perfect image for Brandon's usual expression around Eliot: like it was all a big game to him, but one that wasn't quite as fun as he wanted it to be.

"Did they know each other back in L.A., do you know?" I asked.

"Probably. It's like a small town, pretty much everyone knows everyone else. I think they were in a few of the same shows."

"What do you think about Evan?" I asked. Tony looked at me thoughtfully, and I had a feeling she already knew where I was going with this.

"You mean, what do I think about that little Brandon-Evan-Eliot love triangle that was brewing, now conveniently much easier - at least for Brandon - with Eliot out of the way?" Tony replied. "I think that Brandon might be something of a drama queen, but killing someone over a week of jealousy might be going too far, even for him. Otherwise, I have a feeling the trail behind him would be littered with bodies."

"I know," I sighed. "That's the trouble with anyone's motive. We were only here with Eliot for a week or so."

"So you think it must be related to someone who knew him from home?" Tony asked.

"Maybe. Probably. I mean, I'm trying not to leap to too many conclusions," I said, trying to sound more reasonable than I actually felt, with lists of suspects running through my head all night. "But if it is something related to Eliot in L.A., what did you think about all the plagiarism talk the other night?"

"I think that Brandon loves a good story," Tony said. "And I would normally discount it a bit, but I'd actually heard it myself, when all that was going down with the residency a few months ago. Plus, I think it says a lot that Rachel wouldn't admit it had been her work that was copied." I'd filled Tony in on the rest of my searches on our way over here. I'd gotten a bit of side eye when I got to the part about bumping Rachel's computer on, but thankfully, no further questions.

"Exactly," I replied. "It may sound extreme, but I think it gives her a perfect motive: Eliot beat her out for a residency program, using her own work." We both considered what that must have been like.

"It's pretty cold," I added. "I may not kill over it, myself, but I would definitely be wishing some pretty terrible stuff on whoever had plagiarized me."

"I bet," Tony said, laughing.. "But do you think that Rachel really has the strength - physically or emotionally - to kill someone the way that Eliot was killed?"

"I think if we're adding you to the suspect list, then we can't rule out Rachel based on physical strength alone," I said, a bit uncertain. I was still finding the line where it was okay to make comments about Tony's wheelchair, and what was plain rude.

"Touché," Tony nodded. "And we've never seen what her temper might be like. For all we know, she's a regular Hulk." I grinned, picturing Rachel - just a couple inches taller than I was - the size of the green giant.

"There's also Ryan," I said reluctantly.

"The owner of the murder weapon? Yeah, not a great look for

an innocent person," Tony replied. "Do you happen to know if anyone actually saw him in the woodshop that night?"

I shook my head. "Jenny told me that she heard someone leaving the house that night - or at least leaving their room - and assumed it was Ryan."

"Do they have rooms right next to each other?" she asked.

I had to shake my head again. "No, across the hall. She was pretty adamant it was him, though," I replied.

"But in reality, it probably could've been anyone," Tony said with an eyeroll.

"Yep. And then there's the thefts," I said with a sigh. I laid out my theories about the two likeliest connections between Eliot's death and the thefts: either he found out who was stealing the objects and was killed for what he knew, or he was actually the thief, and killed in retaliation.

Tony was appraising me skeptically. "I could believe he was killed for finding out who the thief was, I guess," she said. "But would you really kill someone for stealing your roll of canvas? I don't buy it."

"No, I don't really either," I agreed. "I mean, I still think it's worth having as a possibility. But I agree, it's more likely that he was killed for finding the thief. Which means that it's probably still worth looking for the stolen items: if we can find them, maybe we can find our killer." I had to admit, I was really loving the new "we" here. Sneaking around, searching rooms: It was honestly pretty nerve-wracking to be at it alone, without someone to stand lookout. But two people sneaking around? Now that was a party.

Tony was nodding. "Agreed, we'll continue the search," she said. "Also, I think we need to fill in way more background info on Eliot. If he was killed for something related to his life in L.A., then we obviously need to know more about his life there. Ideally without letting anyone know we're looking into it."

"I was thinking the same thing," I agreed. "Did you notice the little library a few streets over? I think that'll be a good spot for some private research."

Tony was silent for a few moments, looking thoughtfully out the window next to us.

"I think we also need to find out more about the night Eliot was killed. Who was where, doing what, that kind of thing," Tony paused. "Is that something you've done before, in this kind of…experience? Interviewing people?"

A series of images flashed through my mind, one uncomfortable conversation after another, at parties and in studios and cramped faculty offices. I don't know that I would've called them interviews at the time, but I had to admit now that that was, in fact, exactly what I'd been doing.

"Yeah, but I think seven people is too many to work through.

At least quickly," I said. "I think it would go better if we split everyone up between us."

"Eight people, actually," Tony pointed out. "I don't think we should even rule out Madeline Berry, at least not yet. Isn't it usually the housekeeper in the library, with the candlestick?" The waitress came over to clear our dirty dishes, pausing as she obviously overheard Tony's last comment.

"Madeline Berry?" The waitress asked, still leaning half over the table. "Are you ladies at that artists' residency program? Where that poor boy was killed?" We had to admit that yes, we were.

"Do you know Madeline?" Tony asked politely.

"Of course, everyone here does. I was so happy when Maddie came back to town," she said. "I just hope this isn't too much for her."

"Came back?" I asked, hoping this sounded like a casual question and not a demand related to wondering whether it really had been the housekeeper with the candlestick.

"Oh, yeah," the waitress replied. "Maddie grew up here. I went to high school with her." I was about to ask another question when we were interrupted by a couple at the table next to us who were waiting to order. From the look on her face, Tony had an unanswered question or two as well.

We waited until the waitress had finished taking the couple's order and walked back to the kitchen. Tony leaned forward, keeping her voice quiet.

"Why didn't Madeline tell us she was from here?" Tony whispered. "I asked, the first day here, if Madeline was from Vermont. I said I wasn't used to all the snow. She only said that she'd been at Winterbrook for a couple of years."

"Okay, so definitely eight people to interview," I confirmed. "I'll take Madeline, plus Timothy, Brandon, and Rachel. You okay with the other four?" Tony nodded. We agreed that we'd take the rest of the day and most of the weekend to talk to everyone. I wasn't sure how much farther today's conversation had really gotten us, but it definitely felt like a relief to talk through everything with someone else (especially someone who didn't think I was crazy). I could already see a mini investigation board forming in my mind, a web of string starting to connect a series of pictures of everyone here. Did I watch way too many mystery shows set in police departments? Yes, absolutely. Was I regretting it? Not right now.

*

We got back to the farmhouse just before lunch. Tony went off to the studio, claiming to do her best thinking while at work painting. I headed to the kitchen, hoping to find Madeline and check the first interview off my list.

"Hi!" I called brightly as I walked into the kitchen, a room that had clearly always been the heart of the old house. Although renovated at some point, the kitchen still had its old, beautiful, wide floor planks and original molding, with old single pane glass windows looking out onto the backyard.

"Just here to make some tea!" I said, chipper as could be as I filled up the tea kettle and tried not to look too inept as I struggled with lighting the old gas stove.

"Of course, help yourself," Madeline replied, without bothering to look up from the dough she was working on. I watched as she repeatedly slapped it down onto the counter, picking the dough up and hurling it down each time with such force that I worried for the thin glass in the window next to her. What had been a charmingly New England attitude, full of quiet reticence and calmly knowledgeable, was now suddenly suspicious. Funny how a dead body could do that.

"Must be a ton of work to cook for this many people all the time. Have you always worked in kitchens?" I asked.

"No, actually," Madeline answered. "But I did work in hospitality." I waited for more details but it seemed none would be forthcoming. I kept a polite smile on my face, sitting through the awkwardness as I waited for the tea kettle to come to a boil. I didn't know which would happen sooner: that a watched pot would boil, or that Madeline would suddenly spill her life story to me.

"Ah, cool. So you just wanted to come back home, then? Is that why you took this job?" At this, Madeline paused for a split second, still wrist-deep in bread dough. She quickly resumed her kneading.

"Yes, I'm from Vermont originally," she said, shooting me a quick quizzical glance. Again, it seemed like that was all the information I was going to get.

"Well, this must be a great job, usually. Nice and quiet out here," I said, guessing that that was exactly how she liked it. Madeline smiled but stayed silent, the continued sound of kneading filling the room.

"I'm sure this is the first time anything like this has happened," I continued.

"Yes, of course it is," Madeline said, frowning. It had briefly crossed my mind that she might be the one connected to the thefts, but I had to quickly admit that seemed unlikely. If thefts routinely happened here, I'm sure the story would get out or someone would connect the dots, eventually. After all, only one person was here all the time.

"Your tea is ready," Madeline said, snatching the kettle off the stove just before it whistled. She poured a cup of tea quickly, sliding it over to me. It couldn't have been more obvious that she wanted me to leave than if she'd swatted me out of the kitchen with a broom.

"Great, thanks! See you at lunch, I guess," I said, making my exit quickly and retreating to the dining room.

I somehow made it through lunch while only half listening to the conversation around me, everyone coming back boisterous and giddy after a morning of work. I smiled at Brandon's antics, even laughing at some story Jenny was telling me about an ex-boyfriend who now worked at MoMA and had recently damaged a priceless sculpture, but my mind was elsewhere.

I didn't think my conversation with Madeline could've gone much worse and I had no idea how I'd be able to approach her again, such that she'd actually want to talk to me. I didn't think I'd ever met anyone who was as unforthcoming as she had been. Ordinarily, I might not have even noticed, just chalking her attitude up to being an introvert or liking her privacy. Now, I had to wonder what she was hiding. I know, that doesn't seem especially fair. But in light of everything that had happened, you'd think that Madeline would be a bit more open and, you know, willing to share at least enough information to make it seem like she was an unlikely suspect. All I knew was that Madeline had lied about where she was from, didn't want to share any information about her previous work, or why she was here. I could mentally hear Steph admonish me: *This woman doesn't owe you anything! She's not required to tell you her life story.* Maybe not, but I did wonder if Madeline had been any more open with the police than she'd been with me. I regretted not listening to Steph sooner, although I still didn't see how one could ever really make friends with Detective Peters.

I looked up, realizing that everyone was filing out and I was suddenly sitting alone at an empty table. If Tony and I were going to stay under the radar, I'd have to keep up the pretense of continuing to work, and join the others in the studios.

*

I found Timothy hard at work, tucked in the back of the studio building. Luckily, Evan was playing some podcast in his studio at the front of the room, and it seemed like everyone was listening, rapt, to the interview. I'd be able to talk to Timothy without anyone overhearing. I hoped.

"Samantha," he said with a nod, acknowledging my presence. I let the name go without comment.

"Hey, Tim," I replied, knowing he preferred Timothy. Okay, so not entirely without comment. I know, I know. You're probably supposed to keep your suspect on your side during an interview and not immediately antagonize them, but I couldn't help myself.

"How's it going?" I asked, watching while he loaded up a palette knife with a verdigris paint, adding the dark green over the wash of yellow ochre already on his canvas.

"Not bad," he said, not looking up.

"Recovered from your sketchbook getting stolen?" I said sympathetically. "That sounded tough."

"Yeah, I'm sorry about that. I definitely overreacted," Timothy said, continuing to stripe the canvas with the sharp edge of his palette knife in even, maybe alarmingly firm, strokes. The scraping noise was starting to set my teeth on edge.

"It was just a surprise, you know?" he continued. "But really, the book is filled with junk." I nodded, leaning back like a casual listener and not someone hanging onto every potentially suspicious word. I moved aside a large jug of turpentine and perched on the work table just behind him.

"You must have lost a lot of work, though," I said.

"It was just filled with the interior ramblings of someone who could probably get out a lot more," Timothy said, looking over his shoulder at me with an appraising expression that suggested I could probably stand to get out a lot more too. I laughed obligingly.

"Not much nightlife out in Western Mass, huh?" I asked with a grin. Really, I was picturing the spare interior of Timothy's room here, the spartan life it seemed to suggest. Sure, it may be that he just packed light. But I think it took a certain personality or lifestyle to be comfortable in a room that plain and frankly empty.

"Just enough," Timothy said with a grin.

"I'm sure you work a lot," I said, with a hint of a question.

"As little I can," Timothy laughed. "I freelance for a few different places. Mostly art handling, some crating and shipping. But I try to keep as much time open as I can for my own work."

"Of course, yeah. Always a struggle," I replied truthfully. I was always curious how other artists actually managed this, balancing their artistic work with the reality of needing a job. Of course, some people - at times, it seemed like everyone except me - had some kind of family money to rely on. But from his spare belongings, I doubted that was Timothy's case.

"Sucks that you never found that sketchbook though. Or did you?" I asked, hoping my tone was still casual.

"Nope," Timothy said, returning his full attention to the canvas. Timothy wiped off the palette knife with a well-used rag, picking up a load of dark red vermilion paint and beginning to dab it into the top corner of the canvas. Although it was definitely abstract, I could see a kind of landscape starting to form, a dark forest under a summer sky. Or something like that.

"Ah, well." I heaved a dramatic sigh. "Hopefully it'll turn up soon." Timothy grunted in agreement, fully absorbed back in his work. I made my way over to my studio space, on the other side of the room, casually taking out my own sketchbook and pretending to consider my notes. Sure, they were notes about everyone in the room and their possible motives for murder, but no one needed to know that.

9

Chapter 9

The next morning, Brandon enthusiastically proclaimed over breakfast that what we really needed was to blow off some steam, and proceeded to drag Evan, Simon, Rachel, Timothy, and me to some "charmingly quaint" little antique shop he'd noticed in town. Practically shoving us all into the van, Brandon even managed to sweet talk his way past the pair of police officers who continued to be stationed at the top of the driveway. Although, judging from their bored looks and the way the pair nonchalantly waved us through, we could have told them we were on our way to continue the murder spree, and I doubt they would have minded.

Although charming, the "little" antique shop turned out to be another old farmhouse, three huge floors filled with a dizzying array of different antique dealers. I paused in the entrance, breathing in the familiar musty smells and getting my bearings amid the sea of vintage Pyrex, Fiestaware, and old broken cameras. Simon made a beeline for one such pile, proceeding to go through each camera, methodically checking every one.

The owner, an older woman behind the counter who looked engrossed in her conversation on the kind of corded phone that may have been deliberately vintage or just never replaced in thirty years, merely nodded at us in greeting. Although our reception at the coffee shop had been perfectly pleasant, I had the feeling that the Winterbrook Residency reputation preceded us throughout the small town.

I milled aimlessly from one booth to the next, hoping I'd get the chance to talk to Brandon at some point, an interview still on my list. I mean, I'm sure he'd be happy to talk. The only question was: would I be able to get much truth out of him? Or just another round of gossip? He was a few booths over from me, currently digging through a large bowl of vintage cookware with the expression of an expert who spent most of his weekends in the same position, while next to him Evan carefully examined a stack of vintage aprons.

I was distracted momentarily by the sight of a vintage dollhouse - in an over the top, gingerbread house style - in a booth filled with classic toys, but tore myself away from the tiny furnishings when I saw my chance with Brandon. I noticed him standing alone, appraising a pair of cow-shaped creamers.

"Cute," I said, joining him in the booth. Luckily, the high walls formed by a pair of bookshelves blocked us from the others who were still shopping on this floor. I took another step into the booth, effectively trapping him in the narrow space.

"Yeah, I guess," he said, putting the creamers down again. "But I have no idea who around here is going to pay eight dollars for it." I let this remark go without comment.

"I'm sure you know best," I said. "You have great taste." With anyone else, such blunt flattery would have been far too obvious. But I had a feeling it just might work with Brandon.

"Oh, thanks, dear," he replied absentmindedly, now focused on inspecting a vintage thermos.

"In guys, too," I said, nodding over to where Evan was flipping through a stack of old photos and postcards. "Evan's a sweetheart."

"Yeah, he'll do," Brandon grinned. But I could see genuine feelings there, despite his bluster.

"I guess it's not half-bad that Eliot's, you know…out of the way," I continued, only a bit clumsily. "I got the sense he kind of had a thing for Evan too."

"Oh, please," Brandon snorted. "Eliot was never any real competition for me." Of course, any suspect might immediately reject their own obvious motive for murder. But I did have to admit - especially this close to Brandon's enviously flawless skin and perfectly falling mop of hair - that he was probably right. There had been something a bit weasel-y about Eliot: a long narrow face ending in a pointy nose, half-hidden behind an over sized pair of glasses. Or maybe it had just been his perpetual expression, one of smug confidence, his nose always in the air.

"Does suck that we can't get out of here now," I sighed. Brandon murmured his agreement, still absorbed in his antiquing. I idly picked up a brass candlestick, pretending to inspect the markings on the bottom as I asked my next question, hoping my voice stayed as casual as possible.

"You didn't happen to see anything that night, did you?" I asked. Brandon frowned, his attention pulled away from a pile of colorful Pyrex, and for just a moment, I thought I could sense a split in his usual facade of easy-going charm.

"I'm only asking because I heard someone going out that night, leaving the farmhouse. And I was just wondering if you happened to see who it was? It's hard not to be curious," I continued.

"Well, it's hard to say," Brandon said, finally turning his full attention to me. He leaned over and lowered his voice. "I didn't know what time Eliot died, of course. When we first heard about what happened. But then, when I was talking to the police, and they were asking about this time and that time, I realized - "

"Brandon!" Evan cried, brandishing a set of photos as he strode over to us. "Look at these!" Evan practically pushed past me as he walked into the booth, eager to show Brandon some old family photos that couldn't possibly compete with discussing a murder investigation. But Brandon immediately dropped our conversation, instantly absorbed in the photos. Whatever he'd been about to tell me, it was obvious that it wasn't something Brandon was willing to say in front of anyone else.

My mouth was still half-open, trying to ask another question about what Brandon realized about the night Eliot died, but I could see it was useless. I would have to get Brandon alone again if I was ever going to find out more.

I wandered off without another word, pretending to care about a stack of old wool sweaters in the next booth, not even bothering to make it seem like I wasn't just there to ask about Eliot. I continued down the aisle, not even bothering to go into each booth anymore. It wouldn't have been any use, anyway: All I could think about was what Brandon had been about to tell me.

Around me, Simon was still engrossed in taking apart old cameras, and Rachel was rapidly filling a basket with old linens. Near the back of the store, Timothy was flipping through a stack of paintings, carefully examining the frame and back of each one. He pulled out a particularly creepy painting of two children (are old paintings of kids ever *not* creepy?), gently peeling up a corner of the paper backing to see the back of the frame.

"Yep, that'll do," he said, mostly to himself.

"For what? The trash pile?" Brandon snickered, coming up behind us. Timothy only smiled, taking his purchase over to the counter. Simon joined him, with a small armful of cameras. Even Brandon had found something worth deigning to buy: a frilly pillow embroidered with "Aunt" on it.

We headed outside, about to pile back into the van, when I

hung back.

"I think I'm actually going to hang here for a bit," I said. "Grab some lunch, take a walk around. I can walk back later." Not that I was really looking forward to slogging through the slushy mess along the side of the road the whole way, but compared to the usual inner demons of detective story protagonists, I guess this wasn't much to complain about.

"Suit yourself," Brandon shrugged, already turning on the van, which gave an alarmingly loud rumble. I waved them off and stayed where I was until the van had turned the corner, then slowly headed up the street to the town library.

*

The library was small, set in what must have been an old school building, not much more than one room. But it was clearly well-loved, with high shelves overflowing with books ringing a room filled with cozy reading tables. I quietly slid into a computer desk, trying not to disturb the handful of people scattered throughout the room.

With my mental list of artists ready, I knew I had a few hours of research ahead of me. I cracked my knuckles, stretching, like I was about to enter the ring. I started with the star of the day himself, but unfortunately there wasn't that much out there about Eliot. His death had already made the news, so most of the recent results about him were generic memorials, nothing too personal or insightful. I clicked through several similar articles, mostly published by L.A.-based newspapers or art websites. Each featured a few photos of Eliot's work and the same headshot: Eliot, in black and white, staring moodily into the camera in his studio, an array of paintings laid out behind him alongside well-used supplies, a pastiche of an artist's portrait.

I moved on to his personal website, trying not to smirk at its overwrought, minimalist design. He'd put up images of years worth of his work, which I scrolled through now. Eliot had mostly been a painter and it seemed like he worked in any and all styles: there were large-scale abstract paintings, academically minimalist drawings, and some layered, gestural works I took to be landscapes.

And there, a few dozen images in, was the work that had to have been copied from Rachel. A series of six images showed work that incorporated heavy, dark fabrics, which had been draped over canvases, spilling over the edges and partially obscuring the images beneath; in other works, the image continued onto the fabric wherever fabric and canvas met. I told my inner critic to take the day off. Instead of diving right in to the kind of impassioned - and only occasionally misguided - critique that usually comes from one too many years in art school, I opened a new tab, pulling up images of Rachel's work. I carefully studied each of Eliot's copies, comparing them to Rachel's originals and looking for any that were exact replicas.

I wasn't sure precisely where plagiarism started. In fact, I doubt any artist could say with certainty where exactly the differences lay between imitation, inspiration, flattery, and outright theft. I could certainly see that Eliot's work bore a striking resemblance to Rachel's, although none were exact matches. On the other hand, if he had just beaten me out for a prestigious residency by becoming "inspired" by my work, I don't think I'd have any qualms about calling him a plagiarist.

Zooming back out, I took in Eliot's work as a whole, looking at the whole page of thumbnails. It really was striking how many different styles and methods Eliot seemed to work in, often creating discrete bodies of work that bore little resemblance to one another. Almost as if each body of work had been done by a different artist.

I wondered how many other artists Eliot had copied over the years. Or how I would ever be able to find that out. I sighed, suddenly struck by the magnitude of the task in front of me. It was true that figuring out who killed Eliot - as quickly as possible - was the only way I was going to be able to get out of here soon and back home. And while he had obviously been killed by someone who was also here, the truth was that Eliot had had an entire life back home. The residency hadn't lasted more than ten days before Eliot had been killed. Yet I still couldn't shake the feeling that his death was directly connected to something - or someone - at Winterbrook.

I clicked over to the page where Eliot had posted his CV, hoping my inner critic would at least take a long lunch, if not the whole day off. It was always hard not to feel somewhat jealous when reading a list of other artists' accomplishments, their gallery shows and prizes. I had been sending my work out to galleries all year after graduation, and had only shown in a handful of local and regional group exhibitions so far. Eliot, on the other hand, had shown all over L.A. and received a number of prestigious - or at least prestigious sounding - prizes and fellowships over the last couple of years. I wondered again how long-running Eliot's plagiarism was, thinking that there might be a connection with another residency, just as there had been with Rachel and the program in L.A. I inadvertently let out a frustrated groan as I realized the amount of work it would take to comb through a network of artists who had been at the same residencies as Eliot, and compare their work to his to find any that were overly similar. Actually, I realized, that sounded like a perfect job for a journalist. I started a new email to Arun, detailing my (hopefully manageable) request. You know, just the kind of thing a girlfriend would normally ask for.

Done with his personal website, I skimmed a few of the exhibition reviews that mentioned Eliot's work. It seemed like his paintings had been well received, but none of the reviews I read could be described as "glowing." I allowed myself a small moment of satisfaction at that. What? Even Miss Marple got to have some fun, sometimes.

I took a break to stretch and do a quick lap around the room, walking off the kind of exhaustion that comes from staring at dozens of images. I paused to admire a particularly robust mystery section before settling back in at the computer.

A search for Simon turned up only the website for his commercial work - which was so slickly produced and clearly successful that I had to wonder if it was really a smart idea for him to move away from that work. Would I sell out, if given the chance? Yes, of course. Absolutely. All that meant to me is that I'd be paid to make things, even if those things weren't the high-minded *object d'art* that some artists might have wished to be known for. Of course, I hadn't gotten the chance.

In contrast, Ryan's web presence was minimal, with a few social media profiles that featured mostly photos of a smiling woman I assumed was his wife, often with one or two dogs. He had a simple website where he sold small furniture items, but nothing that could conceivably be linked to Eliot. Unless Eliot was killed because he disliked curly maple side tables.

I worked my way through the next few artists, not finding anything remarkable about Evan or Rachel. I spent a few extra minutes on Jenny, enjoying the sheer exuberance of her work. Her portraits were bright, with richly layered washes of color, often incorporating different abstract patterns and motifs in the background behind the central figure, who was often depicted in a way that one might have called "cartoonish," sort of like a more Pop Art version of Kehinde Wiley's work.

On her About Me page, I noticed a familiar name, and googled: Jenny had been shortlisted last year for a fellowship program based in Michigan, which combined a few months in residency with teaching at a local college. On the fellowship website, I scrolled through the list of awarded artists until I found the year Jenny had been shortlisted.

Well, well. Right at the top of the page was the star of the day. It seemed like Rachel wasn't the only one who'd been bested by Eliot for a prestigious position. And like Rachel, Jenny hadn't ever disclosed that she'd had a previous connection to Eliot. She must have recognized his name immediately - I know I would've known exactly who'd beat me for a big award and really, I swear I'm not even that competitive.

My mind flashed back to our first days here, when Eliot had boasted about the work he'd done in his previous residency. I knew that couldn't have been easy for Jenny to hear. The only question was, had it made her angry enough to kill over?

Obviously, I couldn't answer that question just yet. But I did send a quick text to Tony, letting her know that she might want to ask a few extra questions about this when she talked to Jenny. Her reply was immediate: *On it.* I smiled. It felt good to have a team.

Timothy was the last artist on my list for today (since a quick search for Brandon revealed only that he was, unsurprisingly, something of an Instagram star but otherwise didn't seem to have any connections to Eliot). What was notable about Timothy's search results was mostly what they didn't show. He had no personal website and only one social media account, set to private. There were a handful of exhibit reviews that mentioned his work, but most were from a few years ago; it didn't look like he'd been showing all that recently. Although, I realized, he did have gallery representation - something the rest of us actually lacked, despite all the lists of awards and shortlists.

Timothy was represented by the Albert Walter Gallery, in New York, no less. There was something about the name that seemed to ring a slight bell for me, but it had been a long afternoon of searching and scrolling and whatever it was, I couldn't remember now. I added the name to my list for Arun, hoping I wasn't asking for too much.

I had to wonder what an apparently broke artist from Western Massachusetts, who tried to work as little as possible, had to do to secure representation with a New York gallery. Sure, it could just be that Timothy's work was that good. I pictured the flood of unanswered emails I'd sent out, the photos of my work that I'd spent hours laboring over. However he'd done it, it couldn't have been easy.

I looked up, suddenly realizing that the light pouring in through the old window panes had suddenly darkened, taking on a particularly rosy glow that looked much warmer than it actually was outside. I checked the time on my phone and was greeted by a slew of unread messages. From Jenny: *Bonfire party!!!!* And then a string of texts wondering where I was and when was I coming back, with increasing belligerence and exclamation points. From Tony: *Can you get back here please? You left me alone with these maniacs.* I laughed, receiving a stern look from the librarian as I hurried to gather my things. No worries, Tony. I was on my way.

10

Chapter 10

As I walked up the driveway to the farmhouse, it didn't especially look like a party was going on. The sun had quickly set as I walked home, the darkness falling instantly and totally, bringing a new chill with it. I still wasn't used to the nighttime here, this far from city lights and sounds. I'd used the flashlight on my phone as I'd walked, watching the bobbing beam of light and trying not to feel like an extra in *The Blair Witch Project*.

I walked through the yard to the right of the farmhouse, following a set of footprints around the side of the house, towards the sound of loud voices. As I turned the corner, I was greeted by a large, crackling fire that the other artists had built in the center of the backyard, dragging over chairs and a few large logs (that hadn't yet been split for firewood) to sit on. Madeline was even passing out mugs of what I suddenly, fervently, wished was hot chocolate. My stomach growled as I wondered whether there were any s'mores going around, too.

Although, judging from the clearly drunken laughter, it wasn't just hot chocolate being served.

"Sam!" Jenny cried, getting up from where she sat by the fire and tackling me with a slightly drunken bear hug. I leaned away from her, patting Jenny awkwardly on the back. I wondered how close she'd have to get to the fire for the alcohol fumes on her breath to ignite.

I let Jenny lead me over to the fire, not minding when she forced a mug of what turned out to be mulled cider into my hands, adding a splash of whiskey from a flask she'd had tucked under her long shawl. Across the fire, I could see Tony and Simon engrossed in conversation. From their expressions, it looked like Simon was deep in some technical explanation that only one of them was following. I caught Tony's eye and with an apologetic smile, tilted my head slightly towards the house, in the universal signal that we should get away and talk, and also that I was sorry to have left her alone with these maniacs.

Once safely ensconced inside, I shut the living room door and settled in at the couch, across from Tony.

"How was your afternoon?" I asked. Tony pinched the bridge of her nose, exhaling loudly.

"Well, I had a series of increasingly awkward conversations with everyone about, you know, what reasons they had for killing Eliot and if, in fact, they maybe did kill him," Tony replied. "And by the end of the afternoon, everyone was so on edge they were basically hysterical," she continued. "So

Brandon decided that the thing to do was have a party. With a huge fire."

"Yeah, that makes sense. Sounds like a great afternoon. Very low key," I said, earning an eye roll from Tony. But at least she gave a small smile, too.

"But listen, speaking of Brandon," I said, suddenly serious. "He was about to tell me something, this morning at the antique store. I think he saw something the night Eliot died. Someone coming in or out of the woodshop."

"But he didn't say who it was?" Tony asked. "Do you know if he recognized the person or did he just see a figure, or a shadow or something?"

"I don't know. Evan came over and we were interrupted. He immediately dropped it," I said. Which meant, I realized, that Brandon probably hadn't and didn't want to share this particular tidbit with anyone else. Even Evan. "I have to try and get him alone again."

"Good luck," Tony snorted, gesturing behind me out the window. I turned to see Jenny, Evan, and Brandon in a pile on one of the logs, a blanket stretched across their laps, with Brandon clearly holding court and the others laughing.

"I'll try him tomorrow," I agreed. "How were the other conversations? How was Jenny?"

"Jenny was okay," Tony said slowly. "I asked her point-blank about the fellowship. She claimed it was all water under the bridge. Said she didn't even realize who Eliot was until after everything had happened."

"Do you believe her?" I asked.

"I don't know," Tony replied. "But it was weird: The whole time we were talking, she was stretching canvases. And she just kept stretching them tighter and tighter, really going at it with the staple gun. I swear she even ripped the canvas on one of them."

"So maybe some anger there," I said lightly. "Duly noted. Did you hear anything useful from anyone else?"

"Not really," Tony said glumly. "Simon was on the phone with his wife most of Monday night and didn't hear or see anything. Ryan is, understandably, completely distraught. He knows that everyone suspects him. But he said it was just an accident that his chisel was even in the woodshop at all. He said he just forgot it, because with the thefts and everything, he'd been keeping his tools in his room." I remembered the canvas roll of chisels in Ryan's tool bag, one conveniently missing.

"I believe him," I said. "I mean, I know I probably shouldn't, what with him owning the murder weapon and all. And being the only person here who brought woodworking tools." We both considered this for a moment.

"Even so, I agree," Tony said. "Ryan is just too obvious. What about the library? Did you find anything else?"

"I think Jenny and the fellowship was the big news. But check this out," I said, pulling up a few screenshots on my phone, showing Eliot's portfolio in thumbnails. "I was looking at Eliot's past work. And don't you think each group of work is a little bit...I don't know, *too* distinct?"

"Yeah, wow," Tony said, squinting to see the small images better. "It's almost like this is a bunch of different people's work."

"Exactly," I said, as Tony realized the significance of what she'd just said. "I have a feeling that Rachel wasn't the first artist he plagiarized."

"Do you think maybe Eliot copied someone else here?" Tony asked. "And even if he did, do you think that's a reason anyone here would kill him?"

"Who knows," I replied, genuinely unsure what constituted a good reason for murder, as far as a group of competitive artists was concerned. "As you said, they're a bunch of maniacs."

We both grinned, looking out the window just as Madeline was bringing out another round of hot drinks, to loud cheers. I noticed Rachel off to the side, still cheering along with the others but distinctly on her own.

"Let's get back before the others realize we're gone," I said. "I haven't had a chance to talk to Rachel yet and I think now may be a good time."

"Whatever you say, Nancy Drew," Tony replied, turning and wheeling herself out. I rolled my eyes, but followed without complaint.

*

"Need a refill?" I asked as I sat down next to Rachel, offering a mug of cider.

"Thanks," she smiled, accepting the offer without another word. We sat silently for a few minutes, watching the bonfire steadily crackling. Fairy lights had been set up, strung from tree to tree through the yard, the twinkling lights combined with the fire and stars into a beautiful, wintry mix. If one of us hadn't been a murderer, it might have been a nice evening.

"Can I ask you something?" I said. Rachel stayed silent, but nodded. "What did you do when you found out that Eliot had plagiarized you?" Rachel grimaced, her eyes still on the fire.

"Should I bother asking how you found out?" She said finally, putting down her drink and turning towards me, keeping her voice low.

"I don't think that really matters now," I said, hoping she wouldn't push the point, given the whole "accidentally" nudging her computer on and reading her emails thing.

Rachel sighed. "I didn't really do anything," she said. "I didn't know what there was to do. One of my friends wound up writing to the museum and a few local art critics, but that was about it. It didn't exactly stop Eliot from getting the residency." As she spoke, I tried to detect any hint of malice or bitterness, and honestly couldn't. It was almost as if she was describing something that had happened to someone else, giving me a detached summary.

"Did you say anything to Eliot about it when you got here?" I asked.

"No," Rachel said firmly. "I'm sure he knew that I knew. But I didn't want to give him the satisfaction of knowing how upset I was. He'd already gotten the residency - and the stipend. That was enough." We were both silent for a few moments as I mulled this over. From her tone, it really did sound like Rachel had reasonably put the whole episode behind her and bore no real ill will towards Eliot, or at least not enough that she might act on it. On the other hand, her detached tone could be a sign that it was all in the past to her now - but I wondered what she'd have to do to feel like it was truly over.

"You know, I wasn't the first," Rachel said suddenly. "First artist, that is. Eliot copied anyone, everyone."

"Really? Do you know that for sure?" I asked.

"Oh, please. It's basically an open secret in L.A.," Rachel replied. "Everyone knew someone who'd been plagiarized by Eliot, or who had their suspicions. But no one ever did anything about it."

"Do you know any of the other artists who were plagiarized?"

Rachel shook her head and stood to go, pausing to turn and look back down at me. "Let's just say that Eliot was the last person you wanted to see at your opening," she said, giving a laugh that contained the only hint of bitterness. Rachel walked off towards the house and I didn't bother to go after her.

Instead, I stood and walked off in the opposite direction, heading around the far side of the house for a quiet cigarette. I stood quietly for a few minutes, trying to keep my mind clear, as I stood shivering against the cold. I hadn't realized how much colder it would be away from the fire, and tucked my scarf around me more tightly.

It seemed like the problem with learning more about Eliot's apparent plagiarism was scale: if he worked locally, using mostly artists in L.A. to copy from, then that narrowed the field. But if, say, Eliot just trawled Instagram for photos of other artists' work, then it would be impossible to come up with a list of artists he'd copied from. Any one of us here could have been one of his victims. Although, I wondered, how hurt would you have to be by plagiarism before you retaliated? Would any amount of plagiarism do it, or would you only lash out if, for instance, the plagiarist had beat you for a spot at a prestigious residency using your own work?

I was suddenly jolted out of my thoughts by rustling sounds coming from the edge of the yard, where the neat lawn met the forest and then quickly blended in with a nearby state park. My brain calmly explained that it might be a wild turkey or a few deer, while my rapidly plummeting stomach was convinced it was a coyote. Or did they have bears here? It was definitely a bear.

I didn't stick around to find out. I turned and fled, making a beeline back for the fire and safety, and running directly into Timothy. Like, full on, walking into a glass door that you didn't see was there, running into him.

"Whoa, easy there," Timothy said, grabbing my arms to steady me. "See a ghost?"

No, but probably a pack of hungry bears. A large pack. "Sorry, no. I just…" I trailed off, really not wanting to admit how scared I'd been of a few leaves rustling around. Not a great look for Nancy Drew.

"Just colder than I realized," I finished. Timothy was still holding my arms, his grip firm.

"You look like you could use a drink," he said with an easy smile, finally letting me go. I gratefully agreed as he went inside to find both of us refills.

I was suddenly glad for this only slightly ragtag group, loudly talking over each other and laughing about some story that, as far as I could hear, involved an artists' model and a radiator. They may have been maniacs, but they were far better than whatever was trampling through the forest out there. Relieved, I sank down onto a log next to Tony's chair and happily joined in, content to let both the fire and the free-flowing drinks keep me warm for the rest of the night.

"We should play a game!" Evan announced.

"Like what?" Simon asked skeptically. Somehow, he became even more serious when drinking. I didn't think my suggestion of a fun murder mystery game would be taken well right about now, so I kept silent.

"Where's Brandon?" Jenny cried. "We can't start without him!"

"We didn't even agree on what we're starting," Tony pointed out and was promptly ignored.

"He went inside to get another jacket. I'll go get him," Evan said, extracting himself from the pile of blankets he was sharing with Jenny, listing only slightly to one side as he headed towards the house.

Jenny and Timothy were debating the merits of Cards Against Humanity versus Apples to Apples, when Evan returned, just a moment later.

"It's Brandon," Evan announced, his voice and walk suddenly sober. My mind instantly cleared and I knew before Evan spoke what his next words would be.

"I think he's dead."

11

Chapter 11

"And then there were none," Detective Peters announced gloomily as he slid into the chair across the table from me. This time, the police had commandeered the dining room for initial interviews. Whether or not they wanted us to see the intimidatingly steady stream of crime scene investigators and uniformed officers going in and out of the kitchen, I couldn't be sure, but I knew at least one of us was more comfortable here than in the studio building.

"Well, actually…" I stammered, slightly taken aback at this new side of Peters. Maybe he had a sense of humor after all. "Eight. And then there were eight."

I hadn't realized before how perfectly the residency fit the *And Then There Were None* mold, but now I didn't think I'd be forgetting it anytime soon.

Peters stayed silent, his eyes serene behind his glasses. I had genuinely no idea what he was waiting for from me. A full confession? An undying profession of love? To take his midnight snack order?

Still without speaking, he leaned down to a box next to his chair and placed a plastic bag on the table, turning it towards me so I could clearly see the contents.

"It's a bottle of turpentine," I said, stating the obvious in hope that my saying something, anything, would get Peters to start talking. And here I thought that it was the police who usually worked hard to get suspects to talk.

"Do you recognize it?" Peters asked.

"Well, yeah," I said slowly. "I just said so. It's a bottle of turpentine." The detective continued to appraise me calmly. I wasn't sure why his gaze made me feel so particularly stupid. It might - just might - have had to do with all the mulled cider that was ingested prior to his arrival. In my defense, it's not like I knew he'd be coming.

"Do you know who it belongs to?" The detective asked.

"I think everyone here brought turp," I said with a shrug. "There's only so many brands and sizes you can get. So no, there's nothing so memorable about this particular bottle such that I could tell you who, among ten artists, it belonged to." I was aware that my voice had taken on a defensive edge and took a deep breath. "Sorry," I added.

"We found this in the kitchen," Peters said, finally about to tell me something. "In a cabinet." Or so I thought. Maybe it was just the late hour, but I still wasn't picking up whatever he was laying down.

"We also found remnants of turpentine in a mug on the counter," he continued. "A mug that, it appears, Brandon was drinking from."

"So he was poisoned?" I asked. No one except Evan had seen Brandon, who'd been found lying in the kitchen. Evan had taken one look and immediately came running back outside, so no one knew yet any of the details.

"You don't know who this belongs to?" Peters asked again, ignoring my question. I'll take that as a yes, thanks Detective.

"No, I really don't. Everyone has some," I replied, remembering the day Jenny had found me upstairs, looking through everyone's room, and emerged from her own room with the bottle of turp.

"But that's probably why the killer left it in the cabinet for you to find so easily," I said, thinking out loud. They wanted it to be obvious that the murder weapon could have belonged to anyone. A complete one-eighty from using the chisel, which could have only belonged to one person.

I looked up and realized that Peters was still staring at me.

"I mean, um. You know. If you were a murderer and..." I trailed off. Peters just nodded slowly.

"Tell me about this party tonight. Was everyone there?" he asked.

"Yes, everyone. I got there after it started, but I don't think anyone left from about five o'clock on."

"No one left at all? Not even for a few minutes?" Peters asked.

"Well, no. Of course people got up," I said, picturing the steady stream of bathroom trips, calls for more blankets, and missions to find snacks. I sighed. "Everyone got up at one point or another." Apparently, at least one person got up to commit a murder with a weapon anyone could have owned. Was it a perfect crime, hidden in plain sight? Or just a particularly well-timed one?

"Was anyone gone for longer than a few minutes?" Detective Peters asked.

"No, just Brandon," I confirmed. My eyes fell on the turpentine again. "Did you find any fingerprints? On the bottle?"

"We won't know until the morning," Peters said. His eyes narrowed. "Why are you concerned about fingerprints, Sam?"

"Not concerned. Just curious." I tried a small smile but it made no dent in his expression. We both stayed silent for a moment.

"Is there anything else you have to tell me?" Peters finally asked.

I remembered my conversation with Brandon earlier in the day.

It was obvious that he had seen the murderer on Monday night, maybe going into or coming out of the woodshop around the time that Eliot had been killed. Brandon's room was on the front of the house, with a large bay window that would've given him a perfect view of the yard and outbuildings. Clearly, he had confronted the killer, maybe asking about what they were doing in the woodshop that night. And the killer had not taken the question well.

It was obvious to me, that is. But did I need to make it obvious to Peters?

"Like what?" I asked, stalling for time. Peters shrugged.

"Anything else that might be relevant." Like the only conceivable motive for Brandon's death?

"Nope, I don't think so," I said. In my defense, I wasn't even sure that Peters would believe me if I told him about what Brandon had said. For all I know, the detective would think I was just making up some story to throw him off the real trail - a trail that would lead to me as the number one suspect.

Or, at least, that's the excuse I'd like to stick with.

"Okay, Sam." Peters didn't stand, but nodded at me in dismissal. "You can go. But if you do think of anything else, you need to let us know. Immediately." If it turned out Peters was a psychic with flawless mind-reading abilities, I wouldn't have been surprised.

I couldn't get out of there fast enough.

*

I shut the door behind me, once again thankful that I was the only person here interested in spending any time in the old pottery shed. Sure, it was kind of creepy and a little bit scary at three in the morning. And no, I hadn't noticed before that ominous click as the door closed, all coffin-like. Or the way the moonlight poured through the one small window, casting ominous tree branches onto the walls.

Still, it was private. And once the light was on, not quite as creepy. I mean, definitely still very creepy. But somewhat better. I took a deep breath of the musty clay smell. Much better. I took out my phone and dialed.

"Why are you waking me up?" Stephanie demanded as she answered the phone.

"Sorry, I know it's really late," I said apologetically. "Or really early. But I had to talk to someone."

"What happened?" Steph asked. I was silent for a beat too long, figuring out how to tell her about this new death. "Samantha!" Steph added menacingly. "If you do not tell me right this minute why you needed to call and wake me up at three a.m., I'm hanging up."

"Someone else was just killed. Brandon," I blurted out.

"Did you call the police?" Yes, Steph. Although maybe it wasn't crazy of her to think that I would've called her first in the event of finding a dead body.

"So what happened?" she asked.

"Someone poisoned him. With turpentine."

"Of course they did," Steph snorted. "Sorry, not trying to be harsh. But I have to wonder how many times I'm going to be woken up in the middle of the night and reminded of all these ridiculous ways that art can kill." Actually, that would've been a great title for a book series. *Art Can Kill.* You know, if I had a Watson-like assistant who wanted to write books about me. But I didn't think now would be a great time to suggest such a venture to Steph.

"The thing is, Brandon told me earlier in the day that he had seen someone on the night Eliot was killed. I mean, not in so many words, exactly," I added. "We were interrupted before he could tell me who it was or anything like that."

"Did you tell the police?" Steph asked. Again, I was silent for a beat too long. "Samantha! You absolutely have to tell the police. I mean, is there any other reason someone would have wanted to kill Brandon?"

"No," I said quietly. "I mean, maybe. He could have - "

"Sam! No," Steph cut me off. "He saw too much, said too much to the wrong person, and was killed. It's obvious. Isn't that, like, half the reason people are always getting killed in those books you read?"

"Those books - " I started, before realizing I was getting defensive about the wrong thing.

"Okay, yeah," I said with a sigh. "I'll go to the police about it."

"Tomorrow." Steph said with finality.

"Yes, tomorrow. Sure," I agreed. Since today was technically Sunday, at least that would give me until Monday.

"In the meantime, maybe don't tell anyone else there about this. About what Brandon told you," Steph said. "Just get some sleep. Go straight to the police tomorrow. If you don't," she added, "I'm coming up there and dragging you in myself. And you know I hate having to drive in the snow." I groaned, picturing a particularly memorable blizzard after which Steph and I had gotten stuck in a parking space downtown, the wheels spinning uselessly while she screamed a string of obscenities I won't repeat. Not an experience I wanted to relive just now.

"Really Sam, please be careful," Steph added, suddenly serious.

"I'm trying, really," I said, promising to keep her updated as we signed off. I put the phone down, suddenly feeling very alone in the old shed, the shadows no less creepy than they were before. I may not be able to sleep, but I suddenly wanted very much to be anywhere but here.

12

Chapter 12

After not getting to sleep until nearly four a.m., I didn't wake up until almost ten on Sunday, something I hadn't done since I was a teenager. I know, college students are all supposed to be lazy and hungover, but I always had at least one part-time job to get to. And two female roommates to compete with for our one bathroom.

I came downstairs, only to find the farmhouse already deserted. Everyone must have scattered, off to their own studio spaces. Even Madeline wasn't at her usual post in the kitchen. I poured myself a cup of lukewarm, leftover coffee and took it to go.

As I entered the studio building, it was like walking into a library. A very old, very quiet library, where not only the librarians but all the other patrons would shush you. I wasn't sure which had the more sobering effect on everyone this morning: being hungover or the fact that there had been a second murder. Either way, almost no one looked up as I walked in and quietly made my way over to Tony's studio space.

"Should I even bother saying good morning or just ask what the hell you think is going on?" Tony asked in greeting. She was working on a maquette of a new installation, with foam core, different fabrics, and a few different tubs of acrylic gels laid out on the work table in front of her. Not even bothering to put down the hot glue gun, Tony continued.

"I mean, obviously the two deaths are connected," she said, keeping her voice low. I peered around the corner of the temporary wall, but everyone else was working, no one looking our way. "Do you have any ideas yet? I was hoping you somehow knew more than I did. You know, being the expert and everything."

I wasn't sure whether this was exactly a compliment. Deflecting her question, I instead asked, "What do you think about alibis for last night?" Lying there, trying to fall asleep last night, I'd replayed the whole night's events in my head. As I'd told Peters, every single person had gotten up at one point or another and gone back into the house, meaning that anyone who had gone in right before Brandon or during the time he was gone could have done it. Except - I was pretty sure - Ryan and Simon, who hadn't left the fire at around the right time.

"No one has an alibi," Tony confirmed matter-of-factly. "I don't see that the circumstances of Brandon's death actually get us much closer to finding out who did it."

"No," I agreed, noticing a bottle of turpentine in the corner of Tony's workspace. "I don't know which is more genius: using a murder weapon that points to only one person, or using a murder weapon that points to everyone."

"Well, at least our killer is covering all their bases," Tony replied.

"Even so, I think it's worth asking around again to see who does have - or thinks they have - an alibi for last night," I said. "I'll take Jenny, you take Rachel?" Tony nodded, implicitly agreeing that these two ladies were currently our top two suspects.

That said, there were a few loose ends that had been nagging at me since late last night.

"Also, we still don't know much more about Madeline than we did on our first day here," I continued. "I think she's worth another conversation too. Clearly, whatever is going on, she's doing a lot of work to keep it covered up." Tony made a noncommittal noise, focused on painting a small foam column, dolloping on globs of a clear acrylic gel mixed with tiny glass beads.

She paused, looking over her shoulder at me. "And there's still the small matter of the stolen items."

"I know," I sighed. "I never found any trace of them. But I agree, we need to look again." Because there was still the distinct possibility that Eliot had been killed for finding out whoever had been behind the thefts. Or, I was starting to realize, for being the thief himself.

We quietly agreed that I would take the outbuildings and the top floor of the farmhouse, while Tony would search the first floor. I slipped out of her studio space, casually looking around to make sure that everyone else was still absorbed in their work. So far, so good. I headed to the back where my own space was, planning to pick up a few sketches before going out to the pottery shed.

Jenny looked up as I passed her studio. "Morning, Sam," she said softly but more or less brightly. Jenny was perched on a stool, a pair of large dark sunglasses on. She sat slouched in front of her canvas, her over sized denim smock swallowing her thin frame.

"How're you feeling today?" I asked, coming in and perching on the work table next to her, careful to avoid the many paint - and yes, turpentine - stains.

"Oh, you know," Jenny replied, pushing the sunglasses up. She blinked in the bright light, her eyes red-rimmed. "Been better." Jenny cleared her throat, returning her focus to her painting with determination. I murmured something nondescript but sympathetic, tilting my head to study the canvas. A woman in a bright pink baseball cap and long black dress lounged against an emerald green sofa, floating freely on a sea of magenta and ochre paislies. If Iris Apfel ever commissioned a portrait, Jenny would be the perfect painter for her.

"Yeah, it was a rough night. To say the least," I agreed. Jenny was adding a series of tiny teal dots to the magenta background, pausing only to absentmindedly wipe her brush on her smock periodically. The smock was a work of art in and of itself: a constellation of brush marks and hand prints layered across the front and back. I pretended to be engrossed in her painting while I considered my next question.

"You didn't happen to see anything last night, did you?" I asked. "I mean, when you got up or went into the house?"

"Did you see me last night?" Jenny snorted. "If I saw anything, I definitely wasn't in any state to realize what I was seeing and definitely not to remember it today."

"Sure, of course," I agreed. "But you did go into the house last night, right?"

Jenny laughed. "What, are you asking me if I have an alibi for last night?" I stayed silent. After a moment, she looked up at me.

"Oh, damn. You really are asking if I have an alibi." Jenny looked at me appraisingly. "Okay, Sam. If you want to know, then no, I don't think I do. I don't know exactly when Brandon was killed, but all I remember is being around the fire with everyone. I'm sure I got up at some point to come in and use the bathroom or something, but I definitely don't know what time that was."

"Sorry, I'm not trying to put you on the spot - " I started to apologize.

"It's fine, whatever Sam," Jenny waved me off, returning to her painting. "Everyone is wondering the same thing. And this time," she continued, lowering her voice, "I have absolutely no idea who did it."

"No, me neither," I agreed, looking around the studio building with a critical eye. Of course, it could still be you, Jenny. But I didn't say that.

*

I was grateful to get out of the studio building and its mausoleum-like atmosphere. The pottery shed was, in comparison, a peaceful but lively space, with bright winter sunlight pouring in and the sound of the wind outside almost soothing. Gone were the spooky tree branches and mystery noises of last night and I almost laughed at the memory of how much I'd scared myself. Almost.

My raku pieces had been fully fired and cured, and were now ready for a second layer of glazes. Each blobby form had turned out a bit differently, despite the fact that they were all fired with the same materials: the dried leaves, seed pods, and twigs had imparted a seemingly endless array of different patterns. I was currently dabbing on a copper oxide glaze, which would become a dark green layer over the mottled black and tan base. There was always something magical to me about ceramic glazes, the way these basic metals and organic materials could change colors and textures just with the application of heat, a piece coming out of a kiln as an entirely different object then when it entered. It was like the way an image on a piece of photo paper instantly appeared when dipped into developer: sheer magic. I think this is at least part of the reason artists do what they do. Only children get to regularly experience this kind of magic on a daily basis.

I was just starting to glaze the third form when my phone rang. I was about to curse the interruption before I saw that it was Arun.

"Hi, Sam, how are you?" he answered. "Steph told me what happened last night." I could almost hear him frowning. I could also hear a level of background noise that told me he wasn't at home right now.

"Are you at the office right now?" I asked, evading his question. "Is work okay there?"

Arun paused, knowing exactly what I was doing. "Do you want to talk about what happened, or just continue to ask each other questions neither one of us will answer?"

I laughed. "Yeah, fun as that sounds, I guess you're right. Can't avoid it forever."

"Really, are you okay?" Arun asked again. "Steph said you didn't sound too good." Et tu, Stephanie?

"I'm okay. Obviously, it wasn't the most fun night…" I trailed off, trying to figure out how to describe the mix of dread, curiosity, and sheer exhaustion I was feeling at that moment. "I still just have to figure out what happened," I said finally. "I just want to come home."

"Well, I'm not sure how much this will help, but I did get a chance to go through those questions you emailed me," Arun said. I instantly started to feel my mood perk up. Unlike most fictional detectives, I didn't have a friendly local police officer or family doctor to assist me. But I would never turn down a journalist's help. I smiled at the memory of working with Arun a couple of years ago, when my friend had died and he was the only one who believed that it hadn't been an accident and who was willing to help me. If we ever got married (and don't ever tell anyone I started a sentence that way), our wedding should probably be puzzle-themed. Or crime-themed.

"From what I could piece together, there were quite a few other artists that Eliot was definitely plagiarizing," Arun was saying. "I found four whose work matches up more or less one-to-one, all of whom Eliot had been at a residency with in the past few years." He read off a list of names to me: Jason Keans, Catherine Michelson, Allyn Hillock, and Alonso Lotti.

"None of those names mean anything to me," I said with a sigh. But I put Arun on speaker while I searched each name in turn, looking through photos to see if any one of the artists looked even remotely familiar. "No, I don't think these people had anything to do with it. I would love to be able to say that I saw all four of them sneaking around the farmhouse looking murder-y, but I didn't."

"Weird sentiment, but I get it," Arun replied. "I don't really think this will be any more helpful, but I also looked up that gallery you asked about, the Albert Walter Gallery?" It took me a moment to catch up with him before I realized Arun was talking about Timothy's gallery. I knew the name had rung some distant bell, but I couldn't remember now why I had asked.

"It looks like your basic New York, blue-chip gallery," Arun continued. "The only thing I could find that might be of any interest is that the gallery was accused of fraud, a few years back. Some client accused them of selling him a forged painting. They found one expert who would authenticate it and one who wouldn't. Nothing could ever be proved for certain, and eventually the whole case was dropped." Arun paused and I could hear him on the computer in the background, scrolling through his notes. "It doesn't look like the case hurt their business. At least from their website. And there have been no other news stories about the gallery since then."

"Well, thanks for looking into all that for me," I said with a sigh. "I honestly don't know what that has to do with Eliot, but at least it's one less unanswered question." I guess. At the very least, it explained what I was trying to remember that day in the library.

"I'm sorry, love, I wish I could be more helpful," Arun said. From the noises in the background, I could tell he wasn't the only one in the office today, spending his Sunday afternoon at work.

"It's always helpful," I replied, and meant it. "I know you're busy there. How's the case going?"

Arun groaned. "Going into the legal equivalent of overtime." He gave me a rundown of the week's courtroom events in the trial he was still covering, which had begun to capture the city's attention. I knew it was a huge break for Arun, but I couldn't imagine the pressure he must be under.

"I'm so sorry I can't be there with you," I said, imagining how nice it would be to be able to make Arun dinner after work, listen to him talk about work in person. Actually, given how bad my cooking is, it was probably better for Arun that we weren't talking over dinner right now.

"Are you kidding? I'm sorry I can't come up there right now," Arun replied.

I did my best to reassure him, making a few dumb quips about all the weapons just in the pottery shed that I could use to defend myself against the killer. Maybe not the most reassuring tactic I could take. In fact, as we hung up, I shuddered at the thought of having to defend myself, period, weapons at the ready or not. Great job, Sam. Very reassuring.

*

Bright and early Monday morning, I was ready to stay true to my promise to Stephanie. A little too bright and early, for my taste, but, I figured, best to get this conversation with Detective Peters over with as soon as possible. About, you know, how I had withheld major evidence from him when directly asked whether I had any evidence to offer.

Plus, after more or less successfully avoiding everyone else for the rest of the day yesterday, it would be nice to continue my streak and get away from the farmhouse for a while. The tension in the house was palpable, everyone eyeing everyone else with barely disguised suspicion. It was understandable, but didn't make for great breakfast conversation.

I'd decided to walk, despite the freezing temperatures. I texted Tony as I walked down the rutted shoulder, as if this was some blind date and I needed at least one other person to know my whereabouts: *On my way to talk to Detective Peters. If I'm not back by ten, assume I've been arrested.* She replied with a thumbs up and one of those smiley faces that's either laughing or crying. I continued typing, letting Tony know about my conversation with Jenny the day before and how freely she'd admitted to not having an alibi. Tony confirmed that Rachel had said more or less the same thing: *Rachel didn't have an alibi either. Was offended I even asked. Thought she was going to throw her coffee in my face. But she just did that hair flipping thing and stalked off.* In fairness, I could imagine the blunt way Tony had probably phrased the question to Rachel. I'm sure there were plenty of innocent people who would react that way to being asked about their whereabouts while a crime was being committed. Right?

I mulled this over as I walked the rest of the way into town, trying to avoid the slushy spray kicked up by each passing car. On the one hand, both Jenny's and Rachel's reactions to the alibi question seemed natural. On the other hand, either could have been cover for something far more suspicious. I pictured Stephanie's reaction to the problem: she would probably just condemn them both on the spot, with no further questions. And regardless of the fact that there was only one murderer. Unless...

The police station came into view, just down the street, mercifully cutting me off before I could spiral any further. I steeled myself for the conversation I was about to have, trying to feel prepared to meet the unflinching gaze of Detective Peters. So I was a bit over prepared for the alarmingly cheery officer on duty at the front desk, who assured me it would be his pleasure to show me up to the Detective.

As I waited outside Peters' office, I tried hard to stay calm. I was just a regular, non-suspicious person, there to share some pertinent information in a case, like any good Samaritan would. Not someone who was somehow subjecting themselves to being suspect number one just by showing up. I shifted on the hard, blue vinyl chair in the hallway. Even my squeaky shifting sounded suspicious.

Finally, Peters waved me into his office. If I thought that Timothy's room was monk-like, it had nothing on Detective Peters' office. The walls were bare except for a couple of framed awards and a few photos that showed Peters with a series of older white men who I assumed to be various mayors and officials. The window, showing a charming view onto the parking lot, didn't even have blinds or curtains, and the sill was home to one lowly plant, that was in some indeterminate state between dead and alive, or dead and almost dead. Very reassuring.

"Good morning, Samantha. What can I do for you today?" Peters sat back in his chair, steepling his fingers. I felt like I was in the principal's office.

"Yes, thanks for seeing me. I mean, good morning." Great start so far, Sam. I cleared my throat, trying to sound more official. "I actually just wanted to check in and see how the case was going." What? I was definitely going to tell him about the fact that Brandon saw the murderer, who then definitely killed Brandon, but while I was here, I may as well see if I could find out anything. "We're all getting pretty anxious, stuck here. Some of us are far from home, you know. So it would be helpful to get any kind of sense of when we might be able to leave," I continued.

The detective didn't say anything, just looked at me quietly for a beat too long before speaking.

"I've been doing some reading about you, Ms. Green," Peters said, gazing at me with that unnervingly steady look of his. He shifted the papers on his desk, pulling out a print out of a news article - unfortunately, the headline and photograph, even from this upside down angle, looked all too familiar. "I know all about the deaths in Boston and you're…" he paused. "Involvement."

I tried hard not to move, to keep my gaze as steady as his. Peters could at least have the decency to show some satisfaction or enjoyment at how obviously he was making me sweat.

"And I want to be very clear with you: You are absolutely not to have any involvement here. You are not going to interfere with my investigation. And you are not going to come down here and try to pump me for information that you're not privy to," Peters continued.

He looked at me in stern admonishment and I suddenly realized, this guy was barely older than me. Maybe thirty,

thirty-five max. So sure, he was a police detective and all, but what did I really have to be scared of here?

"You're a suspect just like anyone else," Detective Peters intoned. Okay, so there was that. But still. I drew my shoulders back, feeling my resolve returning.

"Of course, Detective, I completely understand," I said, shaking my head as if at my own impertinence. "I have no intention of getting in your way." I stood, gathering my coat and taking a few steps towards the door before spinning around.

"But there was just one thing," I paused. Can't say I hated the dramatic effect. I guess the writers on *Colombo* had the right idea. I rushed on before Peters could even finish rolling his eyes. "Brandon said something to me. On Saturday morning, before he was killed. Brandon told me that he didn't realize it at the time, but he saw someone on the night that Eliot died. Someone who was going into or out of the woodshop at around the right time."

I don't know what reaction I was expecting, but true to form, Peters didn't have the decency to look even mildly surprised.

"If you believe this is so significant, why are you only coming to me with this now?" he asked.

"Well, I mean…" I faltered. Because I was intent on solving this way before you, obviously. Would he believe that I thought the police didn't work on Sundays? "I didn't realize its significance at the time. In my defense, it was two in the morning. I wasn't exactly thinking clearly. But now I can see how important it is."

"Can you?" Peters asked, barely making it sound like a question. I let the silence lie there. Nice guy. I'm sure he was very popular at the local cemetery, or wherever he hung out.

"I just thought you should know," I said with finality. I turned to go, not bothering to wait for him to say another word. See, Steph? I thought. It was pointless trying to work with Peters. If he didn't believe that my conversation with Brandon was significant, I would just have to prove him wrong.

13

Chapter 13

If I thought that the tension in the house was high when I left, it was nothing compared to how it was when I got back. I walked into the dining room, where everyone usually gathered for a mid-morning coffee break about now. But today's break may as well have been a funeral. The atmosphere in the otherwise cozy dining room was icy.

"Hey, guys…" I said uncertainly as I poured myself a cup of coffee. No one was speaking. Poor Ryan looked about as morose as I'd ever seen him, and Timothy was staring into the depths of his coffee like it held the secrets of the world. I almost asked who died, then thought better of it.

I slid into a chair next to Tony, shooting her a quizzical look. She only frowned in response, but Jenny had seen the look and replied for her.

"Ryan's hide glue was just stolen," Jenny announced. Everyone else was still studiously avoiding each other's looks.

"That sucks. I'm sorry to hear that, Ryan," I said, turning towards him. "Was it expensive?"

"Kind of," he said eventually. "It was high grade. So almost forty dollars - "

"It's the principle of the thing," Jenny cut him off. "I thought this would have ended. When…" she faltered, trailing off.

"When Eliot died?" Rachel filled in. "Did everyone assume that he was the thief?"

"He still could be," Evan offered.

"And the killer only wants us to think that it wasn't him," Jenny agreed. Or that the thefts and deaths have been unrelated. I tamped down on the chills climbing up my spine as I considered a killer with a message for us. Or for me, in particular, if the killer knew that I was the one searching for the stolen objects.

"Let's not get too carried away," I said, my voice louder than I'd intended as I tried to calm myself down as much as anyone else. "It's just more missing supplies. It's not a murder."

Jenny sipped her coffee, her silence pointed.

"Yeah, I've had enough," Tony agreed, starting to wheel herself away from the table. "Ryan, you probably just mislaid it and we're jumping to conclusions. Getting ourselves all worked up over nothing."

"Exactly," I said, hoping I sounded more confident than I felt. I mean, I didn't believe a word of it myself. I knew already how I'd be spending the rest of my day: continuing to look for the stolen goods.

"I'm sure you're right," Ryan said, standing to go. "We should all just forget about this. I'm sure it'll turn up."

Without (much) further complaint, everyone else left, too, splitting off for the various studios. Partly to keep up appearances, and partly because it was a small, manageable space that would be easy to cross off my list, I headed out to search the pottery shed.

*

Did I say small and manageable? I should have said cluttered and packed. Overflowing, even. The small space had shelves on three walls, all of which were crammed with bottles of glazes, old and occasionally broken work, and all manner of sculpting tools. I hadn't exactly helped matters, either, spreading out my own work on the one work table, an old behemoth caked in layers and layers of clay and drips of glazes, currently holding not one but three buckets of water and a smattering of sponges, wooden ribs, and other shaping tools. Even the floor was covered in years' worth of spattering wet clay and a more recent layer of twigs and dried leaves, random detritus left from my experiments with raku firing.

However, it would be an absolutely genius place to hide the stolen items, if our thief was especially clever. Hiding it right under my nose, in a mess partially of my own making? Brilliant.

Even if nothing turned up, the idea at least got me to waste an hour of my time searching every nook and cranny in the shed, checking each bottle of glaze to make sure that none were actually the stolen pigments, and even emptying the small cupboard to confirm that our thief had not, in fact, hidden a heat gun behind five years' worth of pottery that had been left behind.

In some ways, I was actually glad I hadn't found anything. The optics of working in the shed with a bunch of stolen stuff? That couldn't have gone well for me.

I was hoping to have more luck in the farmhouse basement. I'd promised Tony I would search it, although I regretted it before I even began. The pottery shed, even with its creepy shadows and spooky sounds, couldn't hold a candle to the two-hundred-year-old basement. I had crept down the basement stairs, pausing at each creaking step to make sure no one had heard me, and was now relying on the watery beam of my phone's flashlight, which failed to illuminate the large space.

The basement ran the whole footprint of the original farm-house. It might have just been nerves, but it certainly felt a lot deeper below grade than the code must be now. The basement still had its original rock walls and dirt floor, basically a glorified root cellar.

I pulled my coat tighter around me, glad I'd thought to bring it down here, where it had to be at least fifteen degrees colder than the rest of the house. I played my flashlight around the room, finding not much more than a few old, rusty tools, a pile of extra chairs, and the newer addition of a few stacked packages of toilet paper.

I was relieved that it didn't take me long to search here, and I wasn't even embarrassed at that. Even your bravest, biggest, toughest person would become a tiny scaredy cat in this classic horror movie space. I mean, the room was lit by a single swinging light bulb. Nothing good ever happened in basements like this.

I didn't even try not to run back up the stairs, completely forgetting about any pretense at being quiet. I burst through the door into the kitchen, practically falling over Madeline Berry.

"Do you need something, Samantha?" she asked, returning to her work at the stove once I'd regained my balance.

"Oh, no. Sorry to bother you. I was just looking for, um. Another stool for the pottery shed," I stammered. Madeline shot me a questioning look, but continued chopping vegetables without another word.

I leaned against the counter, trying to act casual while really just catching my breath.

"Pretty spooky down there," I said truthfully. "I mean, especially after everything that's happened." Madeline gave me a polite smile, murmuring in agreement. We were both silent for a few moments. I was trying to figure out how to ask her anything else, when Madeline put down the knife and turned around before I could say anything.

"All right, Samantha. What is it you want to know?" she asked me. I was taken aback and about to claim I had no idea what she was talking about, but Madeline waved me off.

"Let's save us both a lot of time," she continued. "You were going to come in here and ask me a bunch of questions about Eliot again, or Brandon, and did I see this or think that. So let's just cut to the chase. Ask me anything." Madeline's gaze wasn't even challenging, just calm and coolly appraising me. I think it was actually scarier than if she'd yelled and told me off.

"Okay," I said quietly, deciding not to try and explain myself out of this one. "But I don't want to ask you about Brandon or Eliot." I met her eye, trying to keep my own gaze calm. "I want to know why you don't want to talk to me. About the thefts or the murders, or any of it." I want to know what you're hiding, I thought.

Madeline nodded. "I know it was frustrating for you the other day," she replied. "It was obvious, Sam," Madeline smiled kindly. She took a deep breath, clearly getting ready to tell me whatever the big secret is. I glanced at the large chef's knife on the cutting board behind her and realized at that moment how sincerely I was hoping that I wasn't about to hear a confession.

"I had a bad marriage," Madeline said. She frowned, accentuating the dark circles under her eyes. I had a strong pang of guilt, but knew my curiosity would win out. "He - my ex-husband - was not a bad person. But we were living in New York, running a restaurant together." Madeline looked out the window, considering the cold gray yard as she continued, as if I wasn't even there.

"It's an incredibly stressful business. All late nights and endless customers and staff who quit at the worst possible moment. It put a lot of strain on our marriage. More than we could manage." She turned back towards me. "It did not end well." Madeline said this with a finality that made it clear that I was not getting any further details on this point.

"I came here to be closer to my family and to do something quieter. More peaceful," she said. "I only don't talk about all this, because…" Madeline paused and again looked away from. "It would be best if my ex-husband did not know a lot about what I'm doing or where I am," she said finally.

I was quiet, that pang of guilt having steadily grown the whole time she was speaking. Had I badly misjudged this book by its cover? Yes. But in my defense, that was one hell of a secretive cover given all the murder investigation going on.

*

After groveling in apology to Madeline, who graciously waved me away, I slunk back to the pottery shed with my tail between my legs. So far, for all my searching that afternoon, I'd failed to turn up any missing object and had subjected an obviously innocent woman to retelling a clearly painful episode from her life that had nothing to do with anything that had happened here. Probably in hopes that she'd help me continue the self-flogging, I called Rebecca.

"That sounds tough, Sam," Rebecca said. I'd been hoping that she'd scold me, but Rebecca had so far been sympathetic. I'd caught her at home, after a good day. Rebecca, like me, had gotten a gallery job after graduation, but she also volunteered at a kids' after school art program, and was just getting home from it now. "Do you have any idea when you'll be able to come home?"

"No, not yet," I sighed. In the background, I could hear Rebecca unpacking groceries and could just see it: our kitchen, cozily ringed with fairy lights, a glass of wine on the table while Rebecca cooked dinner. At the moment, I couldn't think of anything better.

"I doubt it's going to be any time soon," I continued. "We just had another theft today. Some hide glue." I ran through the list of missing objects in my head: heat gun, pigments, sketchbook, canvas, hide glue. I was still no closer to figuring out how any of it was related, and said as much to Rebecca.

"What do you mean?" she asked. I smiled as I heard a cork pop. My stomach growled as I wondered what she was about to cook.

"I mean, only some of the objects seem related. The pigments and canvas for painting, right? But then the heat gun seems totally unrelated. And the hide glue is for woodworking."

"Or for sizing canvas," Rebecca said offhandedly. I heard the tap running and then the sound of a package being ripped open. Pasta?

"What did you say?" I was so busy trying to imagine myself into our kitchen that I knew I'd missed something important.

"Oh, just that you can use hide glue to size a canvas. To prepare it for painting," Rebecca replied. "It's what they used to use. In the Renaissance. Or a bit earlier."

"Right," I said slowly. That faint alarm was ringing in my head again, the hairs on my arms rising from what I very much hoped was some kind of sixth sense, and not just the wind pouring in through the drafty door.

"Anyway, have I told you about that kid, Danny? At the after school program?" Rebecca changed the subject, going on to regale me with a sweet anecdote about a particularly precocious eight-year-old, while I laughed along. Although my mind was elsewhere. As Rebecca was speaking and I was still desperately imagining myself at home, in my kitchen and my room, I realized that there was one room I'd missed when searching the farmhouse the other day. A room I'd disregarded, as its occupant was already dead. Eliot's.

*

I wouldn't get the chance to get into Eliot's room until at least after breakfast the next day, a meal that seemed particularly interminable now. It was understandable, since it was day eight of being locked down here, with no end date in sight. And a murderer still on the loose, right in this very house, which made it pretty hard to forget and relax. Safe to say, everyone was freaking out.

Even Evan, normally so quiet and almost mild-mannered, had snapped at Jenny when she knocked into his coffee, spilling some onto the table. Jenny, for her part, had simply rolled her eyes in response, her refusal to engage only making Evan more annoyed. The rest of us sat there silently, the sounds of silverware scraping plates and coffee being slurped setting my teeth on edge.

Finally, Jenny sighed, looking around the table at us.

"I think whoever did it - or even just the thefts - should just come forward and confess already. I don't care what you did or why you did it, but it isn't fair to hold the rest of us here hostage for something only one person did." I could understand her point of view, although it had a certain childlike logic to it. Also, I don't know that I appreciated Jenny's use of the word hostage.

Across the table, Rachel snorted. "Do you think that's really going to happen? How many criminals have you heard of who just waltz into a police station and ask to be arrested?"

"Are you saying that you wouldn't be willing to confess?" Jenny asked pointedly. Rachel erupted in protest.

"Of course I'm not talking about myself. I'm just saying, do you really think that sitting here and asking a criminal to, pretty please, just go and confess is really going to work?"

"I don't, personally," Simon cut in. "But it would obviously help the rest of us a great deal."

"You guys - " Ryan started.

"No, enough," Tony said loudly. She put her mug down like a judge with a gavel. "I know this sucks. Being stuck here is definitely getting old. But there is no point in getting hysterical and blaming each other and pointing fingers. We are going to have to be together for however much longer, so let's just make the best of it. Or at the very least, not make it any worse than it already is." She spoke with finality, no one interrupting her. Around the table, everyone was looking down at their own plates, refusing to make eye contact. We finished the meal in excruciating silence.

I was impressed with the way that Tony had just let loose and let them have it, holding her own against this crowd (of maniacs, as she would say). I said as much to her as soon as we were left alone in the dining room.

"It's not so hard," Tony said with a shrug. "No one wants to be the person who yells at a woman in a wheelchair." She grinned. I had a feeling I would love one of her installations, with its "challenges to viewers' perceptions."

"What's on the agenda for today?" she asked. I leaned over in my chair to peer out the open doorway, but other than the sounds of Madeline doing dishes in the kitchen next door, we were on our own.

"I realized that there's one room we missed in our search," I said, filling her in on my call with Rebecca the night before.

"Didn't the police already search Eliot's room?" Tony asked.

"Sure, but they may have overlooked something." Or so I hoped. It did seem plausible that a police officer may see, for instance, the stolen heat gun tucked away in Eliot's closet and not think twice, since it was just an old tool and this was an artists' colony and didn't all artists keep old, probably stolen, tools in their closet?

Even if she didn't necessarily think I'd find anything, Tony agreed to cover for me while I searched, taking up a sentry position at the bottom of the stairs. After running into Jenny during my first search - and scaring the crap out of myself in the basement yesterday - I wasn't taking any more chances.

Although the police had left Eliot's room locked, it was an old door that only took me a few moments to get opened. What? Half of a potter's toolkit is basically long, thin lock picking tools and if I was being honest, this wasn't the first time my kit had served this particular purpose.

Inside, I shut the door quietly behind me, pausing to get my bearings in the small room. It was hard to tell how neat or messy Eliot had been; it didn't look like the police had put things back in precisely the same spot, as there were now clothes stacked up on the desk chair, the dresser standing open, and books spread out across the bed. I assumed the police would have checked any obvious hiding spots, but took a few moments to check under the mattress and the corners of the closet anyway. I even went through the clothes stacked on the chair (an identical daily uniform of white t-shirt and pristine blue jeans), even if none of the stolen items were small enough to fit into a pocket.

I turned my attention to the books spread out across the simple white duvet, mostly books on painting and drawing: *Lucian Freud: The Drawings; Francis Bacon: The Logic of Sensation; Frank Auerbach* - I sensed a theme and stopped reading titles, instead just shaking out each book to see if Eliot had secreted anything between the pages. You know, like a note that read "I was killed by…"

Finding nothing in the books except a bunch of self-aggrandizing notations, I picked up the last book on the bed, a simple black, hardcover notebook: Eliot's sketchbook. I had no idea what kind of notes or sketches an artist would make if most of their work was plagiarized. A list of names of other artists?

Flipping through the sketchbook, it looked like Eliot had used it partly as a planner ("Need solvents;" "Call M") and partly as intended, filling the blank pages with sketches, some simple drawings and some plans or diagrams of finished work. It was impossible to tell how many of the drawings were original, and how many were copies. I could just picture Eliot walking around a gallery or museum show, sketchbook out, taking down quick drawings of different paintings. On one particularly detailed page, showing what I assumed to be someone else's finished painting, there were even notes about color and paint choices.

"Hi, Rachel," I heard Tony loudly announce from downstairs, Rachel's reply indistinct. I snapped the sketchbook shut and tossed it back down on the bed, racing back out the hall and slowing down just in time to saunter casually down the stairs, offering Rachel a tense smile as we passed each other. Tony was still stationed at the bottom of the stairs and I shook my head at her. No luck.

Although I knew it would take a lot more than luck to figure this out and get out of here. But the truth was, I was exhausted. Exhausted from days of sneaking around and searching dusty, creepy old buildings and thinking about potential suspects. I left the farmhouse and didn't even bother to keep up the pretense of working, walking right past the pottery shed and continuing onto the trail that led into the woods at the edge of the property.

The trees quickly closed in around me, almost instantly cutting off views of the trail head and the farmhouse. That was fine with me. I needed a quiet moment, alone - an afternoon off. I walked slowly, my eyes on the trail and the mottled, brown and white surface of snow and dirt, still-colorful dried leaves poking through. The trail climbed, coming up a small hill (or what should be just a small hill, if you were in better shape than I was). From the top, even at this relatively low perch, I had a beautiful view of the woods spread out below me, with the ruins of an old stone wall spilling through the trees. As a born sculptor, I had actually always wanted to build one of these New England field stone walls, rolling in large rocks and piecing them together with no tools or mortar in sight. I know, it's not exactly a miniature, but I think every sculptor goes through an earth works phase at some point.

I kept walking, trying and failing to keep my mind off Eliot. I couldn't shake the feeling that I had already seen or heard something, something important - something that could explain exactly what had happened to both Eliot and Brandon, if only I could think clearly enough to realize it. I often came to this point in any problem, when I knew - but didn't *know* - the solution.

I stopped walking. As beautiful as it was out here, I knew that I couldn't just race away from the issue like this. There was only one thing for it: a few hours at the pottery wheel, with nothing but the sound of whirring motors and the smell of wet clay around me. At least, I hoped that was the answer.

14

Chapter 14

Although an afternoon off, a few hours spent sitting near-mindless at the pottery wheel, had been great, I'd still woken up vaguely unsatisfied and grumpy the next day. Something in me had snapped somehow. I couldn't even be bothered to make much of an effort getting dressed, just pulling on an over sized flannel shirt over the thermal knit pajamas I had slept in, trying unsuccessfully to cram my uncooperative hair under a beanie.

It seemed like I wasn't alone in feeling like this. Breakfast was an almost silent meal, no one bothering to even try and make small talk. I took out my phone, idly shopping on the website of a local chain of art supply stores. I'd gone through more than half of my remaining supply of clay yesterday and would have to order some more - enough to see me through however much longer we'd be here.

I frowned as my purchase repeatedly failed to go through, my credit card rejected over and over. I groaned, realizing I'd have to move more money from my savings into this account. I was taking unpaid time off from my latest gallery job to be here, and though I'd tried to set aside enough money to cover the whole residency, even with the modest stipend, I guess it wasn't quite enough. I waved off Tony's questioning look as I got up, mumbling something indistinct about less money, more problems.

I trudged up the old stairs, heading to my room to get the login information for my online banking account. I kept a list of passwords on the back of a photograph taped to the inside cover of my sketchbook, a photo that showed Rebecca, Steph and me in our apartment, crushed on the couch together in a fit of laughter. I settled down onto the bed, sketchbook open in my lap and my phone out, ready to place my order, when suddenly I froze.

Of course I kept my passwords in my sketchbook. Because it was one of the only objects that was always, always on me. That no one else would bother to look in. I put absolutely everything in here: passwords, phone numbers, inane thoughts as I walked around museums, quick sketches. I mean, if I was in some kind of drug smuggling operation, I'd probably try and hide it in my sketchbook.

I slowly realized that this is what had stood out to me about the list of stolen objects this whole time: the sketchbook was the only object that could really be valuable, in and of itself. Maybe not for what it was - a basic notebook - but for what might be inside it. Going over the list of stolen objects was almost, I realized with a jolt, like looking at Eliot's portfolio:

like it was the work of more than one person.

I snapped my sketchbook shut, quickly throwing on my coat and not even bothering to change from slippers to boots. Sure, I hadn't been able to find the sketchbook - or any of the stolen items - yet. But there was one building I hadn't gotten to searching yet this week.

I hurried out of the house, darting past the open door to the dining room, where everyone else was still lingering over coffee. I pulled my coat tightly around me as a blast of cold air hit me the moment I opened the door. I didn't even slow down as snow started to fill my slippers, not stopping until I pushed open the heavy barn door to the woodshop.

I paused in the entrance, taking a moment to make sure I was alone in here. Mercifully, Ryan hadn't come in to start working yet. The whole shop was quiet, perfectly still, yet with tools, materials, and plans spread out across four large workbenches, as if an army of busy mice had just stepped out for lunch but would be back at any moment.

I started my search slowly, carefully moving aside bottles and cans of dusty old shellac and stains to check the back of each shelf, heaving up heavy crates of wood scraps to check for any sketchbook shoved underneath. I took particular care to go through a set of metal storage lockers in the back of the woodshop, flipping through lumber and years' worth of discarded old tools. It looked like a perfect hiding spot to me, but no luck.

Suddenly, I remembered what Arun had told me about the defendant in the case he'd been covering, taping the account documents to the underside of his boat. Why couldn't these strokes of genius come to me more quickly? Like, immediately after I found someone who'd been killed. That would've been much more helpful.

I felt underneath the top of each workbench, crouching down to peer underneath. Just as I was about to get discouraged, I bent down at the third workbench, tucked in the far back right corner of the room: bingo. With thick layers of masking tape, a small black sketchbook was pinned to the underside of the table. I carefully peeled off the tape, just enough to free Timothy's sketchbook.

Without a second thought, I sat down right where I was on the sawdust-covered floor and started to flip through the book. Timothy's handwriting was mercifully neat, small letters printed in blocky all-caps that lay centered on each page, around and between drawings and diagrams. His neat handwriting detailed lists of pigment mixes, diagrams of frames, recipes for making sizing out of rabbit skin glue. It was almost, I realized, like reading a catalog of all the other items that had been stolen: pigments for making precise colors, a heat gun for rapidly drying - that is, aging - paintings, hide glue for sizing canvases, which Rebecca had obviously called a historical technique and which I could kick myself for not seeing sooner. There was only one reason to be *this* into historical painting techniques outside of art school. And it was a reason Timothy had killed to protect.

While I was in the middle of all this brilliant reasoning, I heard the unmistakable sound of the door creaking open, heavy boots on old wood floorboards. There was a hopeful split second when I thought it might be Ryan. But then Timothy spoke.

"Have you found it yet, Samantha?" He wasn't even speaking loudly, but his deep voice boomed in the echoey space. "I know you're in here." About the five most terrifying words I could've heard right about now.

My back was pressed against a bin of scrap material and I peered cautiously around the side of it, to see Timothy standing just inside the doorway, moving down the center aisle between the two sets of workbenches. I quietly closed the sketchbook and started to inch myself slowly around the side of the workbench, leaving an obvious trail in the sawdust as I slid on my butt, but hopefully buying myself any amount of time.

But I would have to keep him talking if I really wanted enough time to find some way out of here.

"Where did you hide everything else?" I called out. "You know I was never able to find any of the supplies you took." Timothy's footsteps stopped and he gave a small laugh.

"Does that matter now?" he replied, although his pause seemed to indicate that he was actually considering telling me. "Look up," Timothy commanded.

I did, craning my neck to look at the ceiling twelve or fifteen feet above us. A ceiling strung with thick old rafters. In some places, long boards lay across several of the rafters, an extra storage spot for over sized materials. I groaned as I realized that, like a squirrel, Timothy had cached his supplies high enough up where no one would think to look for them.

"Pretty ironic that Eliot decided to hide the sketchbook here, too," I said. "Did he tell you that?"

"No, but you just did, so thanks for that," Timothy said. "Eliot came in here that night just to taunt me."

I flashed back to Eliot's bragging over dinner a couple nights before he died, his grand plans about his new business proposition. Of course Eliot would have been arrogant enough to talk about forgery in front of everyone, knowing only Timothy would understand.

"What I still don't understand is why you did it. I thought you'd had your breakthrough. Getting gallery representation and everything," I said. Although I was now pretty sure it was a gallery that specialized in forgeries. But still, it was better than I'd done so far.

"Get real, Samantha," Timothy said, the sneer audible in his voice. His voice echoed throughout the barn, bouncing off the heavy metal tools that I was trying desperately not to picture Timothy using as weapons.

"What the hell does breakthrough mean? What is there to breakthrough *to*, anyway? So I can sell a few measly paintings in one gallery. Do you have any idea how much I actually made from those sales?" Timothy continued. I concentrated on the scuff of his shoes along the worn floor, trying to pinpoint his location while I shifted my weight to one leg, ready to spring up at any moment.

"A thousand dollars after taxes. That's it. That's what four paintings got me last year." I heard the footsteps stop and could almost picture him standing there, shaking his head in anger. "How long am I supposed to keep at it for a thousand bucks?" The footsteps resumed.

I risked a peek under the workbench, around the bins of supplies at my back, just enough to see that Timothy was now opposite the table from me. I looked at the slim sketchbook still in my hands, wondering if the corners were sharp enough to be at all useful for self-defense. Although I was sitting in a room literally filled with potential weapons, I couldn't reach anything without making noise and immediately giving away my position.

There was movement in the corner of my eye and I whipped my head around to get a better look: Tony was wheeling silently up the ramp at the door, inching incrementally into the barn. I raised my voice to drown out any sound her wheels might make.

"So when did you turn to forgery?" I asked.

Timothy scoffed. "I didn't 'turn to' anything. That makes it sound like I'm some Dickensian orphan who turned to a life of crime for a bit more porridge. I was offered a job, and I took it. Because it paid a hell of a lot more than a thousand dollars. It was an actual living wage."

I kept my eyes on Tony and my ears on Timothy as I inched down the table, still trying to put more distance between us. I watched as Tony rolled through the doorway, slowly positioning herself behind a stack of milk crates near the front.

"And what about Brandon?" I asked. I wasn't sure what Tony's plan was. I only hoped it was something better formed than mine.

"I was sorry about Brandon," Timothy replied, although with such an obvious shrug in his voice I doubted he was really all that sorry. "But he shouldn't have come to me with all those questions."

"He saw you going into the woodshop that night, didn't he? And he wanted to know what had happened."

"He should have just stayed quiet," Timothy said. I could hear the frustration growing in his voice. I realized with a jolt that I hadn't heard footsteps in a few moments. I looked to my left just as Timothy materialized around the side of the workbench.

"Give that to me," he growled. I leapt up, ready to run for it, but he tackled me, wrestling the sketchbook out of my hands. I tried to get up, delusionally thinking I could go after him, but Timothy had knocked the air completely out of me. I collapsed against the bench, leaning over and desperately trying to catch my breath, when I heard a loud crash.

I looked up, just in time to see Tony's quick maneuver out from behind the crates as she wheeled smack into Timothy, then Timothy tumbling down the ramp at the door, Tony sitting triumphantly at the top.

*

Once again, the flashing lights announced his arrival before I actually saw Detective Peters emerge from his squad car. While Timothy was writhing around at the bottom of the ramp with - hopefully - a few cracked ribs and a broken ankle, Tony had quickly brought me up to speed.

"I called the cops a few minutes before I came out here," Tony said. "When you passed the dining room, I just saw this look on Timothy's face when he saw you. Like he knew exactly where you were going." She shuddered at the thought. "Like a cheetah who's just spotted some poor, dumb antelope." Not sure I loved that metaphor, but given that Tony had just effectively saved my life, I'd take it.

Detective Peters walked slowly through the yard, not even bothering to stop where two officers were currently handcuffing Timothy, despite his loud and belligerent protests of innocence. Instead, Peters walked calmly up the ramp, stopping about halfway up to look at the pair of us appraisingly.

For once, I could return his steady, unwavering gaze, with even my voice calm and strong to make a pronouncement I suddenly knew I'd been saving for exactly this moment.

"And then there were seven."

15

Chapter 15

I was on a bus almost before Detective Peters finally told us we could leave. All I'd wanted was to be back home for days, firmly ensconced in my kitchen while, preferably, someone else cooked for me. As soon as Rebecca had finished literally and metaphorically checking me over for bruises, she consented to allow Steph and Arun over for dinner.

"Seems pretty genius to me," Steph was saying, around a huge bite of lasagna. Rebecca had spent all afternoon cooking, shooing me away when I halfheartedly offered to help. She took restorative comfort food extremely seriously.

"Oh, not really. It's all been done before," Rebecca said, waving her off. "The whole newly-discovered, previously-unknown Old Master painting thing. Or the lesser-known work with dubious provenance that just happens to be sold after generations in one family." She looked up to find all of us staring at her.

"What?" Rebecca said. "It's my favorite sub-genre of true crime books. Plus, I think every serious painter goes through a phase where they think they could be a successful forger." I smiled, picturing Rebecca in some tiny hidden studio, churning out masterpiece after fake masterpiece.

In the days after Timothy's arrest, we had all read the news about the Albert Walter Gallery. How - surprise, surprise - police officers had found stacks of paintings in a storage unit that belonged to Walter; paintings that were now on their way to conservators for authentication. Like a lot of forgery operations over the years, I was sure that some of the paintings would even pass authentication. That was part of the problem with art authentication, no matter how scientific the practice had become. At the end of the day, it still relied on an expert's personal eye.

"Well, Rebecca, when you make it big as a forger and inevitably get caught, I'll be sure to write a flattering profile of you when I cover your case," Arun teased her.

"As far as careers go, it doesn't sound all that bad to me," Steph said. "Plus don't forgers usually get a pretty light sentence? And a great big book deal after?"

I fell quiet as talk turned to whether forgery would really be a fun career path. Ironically, given that he was about to attack me and everything, Timothy's speech in the woodshop had actually had a pretty big effect on me. On the trip home, I thought a lot about what he'd said, realizing that Timothy was right. At least about one thing: what *was* a breakthrough? This whole time after graduating, I'd been waiting for something to happen, convinced I'd get some big break through a combination of working ridiculously long hours, knowing the "right" people (if I could only figure out who they were), and the sheer dumb luck of being in the right place at the right time. But Timothy was right. In all likelihood, I wasn't going to get a big break. Or if I did, it wouldn't look the way I thought it would. Or, more likely, it wouldn't make me anywhere near enough money to actually live on.

Right before I'd left for the residency, I'd gotten a brochure in the mail, casually leaving it out on my desk where I knew I would see it immediately when I got back. The shiny photos of happy students in a storied old building, filled to the brim with both supplies and wise older professors, detailed a relatively new offering at the art school I'd gone to: a one-year graduate program to earn a teaching certificate. It would allow me to teach at the college level, at any art school - something I'd never considered.

My own mom is a fifth grade teacher and still I could never picture myself as some elementary school art teacher - much as I loved my own art teachers at that age, I just couldn't see myself in some kooky, seasonal outfit, happily showing kindergartners how to glue pom poms onto a paper plate. No shade intended, but it just wasn't how I saw myself. But this, the opportunity to essentially do what I already did in my own studio, with other people who wanted to do the same thing professionally. This was something else.

I laughed along as Steph told an extended family story about a five-year-old Arun and a neighbor's puppy. But quietly, I knew I'd just made my mind up. I remembered the new school year feeling I'd had at the start of the residency, how excited I'd gotten just looking at their website. I pictured the brochure, still on my desk. At least school would end better.

www.ingramcontent.com/pod-product-compliance
Lightning Source LLC
Chambersburg PA
CBHW060454300726
48975CB00008B/2509